Rule #13: A lady would *never* initiate advances on a man...

Carly couldn't explain what came over her. "I'm tired of following the rules, Coop," she whispered in a husky voice as she slipped into his arms.

She held her breath, then moaned softly when he traced his tongue over her bottom lip.

"You're bad news," he said roughly as he captured her mouth in a kiss so deep and wet she trembled.

His tongue slid across hers. He tasted like peppermint, and a whole lot like man. Tiny shivers of delight rippled through her. Her nipples beaded against the satin of her bra, the sensation adding to the heat Cooper so effortlessly fanned into a three-alarm blazing inferno.

He lifted his head and she looked into his eyes, feeling a wealth of pleasure ribbon through her at the heat in his gaze.

"Make love to me, Cooper," she murmured. *Another rule broken.* But she was beyond caring.

"Maybe *I* have rules about things like that.... We've only known each other a short time, sweetheart."

The smile curving her sexy, very kissable mouth was filled with sass. "Well, then we better make up for lost time!"

Dear Reader,

Have you ever wondered what you would do if you suddenly found yourself completely free? Would you break every rule you'd ever learned and establish your own laws? Most of us wouldn't dream of doing anything quite so rash, but that's *exactly* what Carly Cassidy does when she runs away from her own wedding and the man she doesn't love.

Carly runs right into The Wilde Side, a local Chicago tavern, and Cooper Wilde, a man convinced Carly has more brass than brains—until she devises an outrageous plan to help him save the place from bankruptcy, and steals his heart in the process.

I hope you enjoy Carly and Cooper's "rule-breaking" romance! And I hope last month you enjoyed meeting Carly's sister Jill and her sexy hero in #793, *Rules of Engagement*.

Happy reading,

Jamie Denton

P.S.: You can write to me at jamie@jamiedenton.net or P.O. Box 224, Mohall, ND 58761-0224.

Books by Jamie Denton

HARLEQUIN TEMPTATION
748—THE SEDUCTION OF SYDNEY
767—VALENTINE FANTASY
793—RULES OF ENGAGEMENT

Breaking The Rules
Jamie Denton

TORONTO • NEW YORK • LONDON
AMSTERDAM • PARIS • SYDNEY • HAMBURG
STOCKHOLM • ATHENS • TOKYO • MILAN • MADRID
PRAGUE • WARSAW • BUDAPEST • AUCKLAND

For The Bunnies

ISBN 0-373-25897-6

BREAKING THE RULES

Copyright © 2000 by Jamie Ann Denton.

1

Rule 1: A lady never cries in public.

FOR THE FIRST time in her life, Carly Cassidy broke the rules, and what had it gotten her? Nothing but trouble, she realized, sitting in her defunct Ford Escort in an unfamiliar city where she knew absolutely no one, and harboring more guilt than any mother—Jewish, Catholic or otherwise—could possibly inflict.

Knowing that she'd disappointed so many people did that to a person, she thought. Her gaze slid to the open doorway of a corner bar. If they had a pay phone, she could call a tow truck. Guilt and regret were tough enough to swallow without adding desperation to her already overloaded emotions. But then again, she had run away from her own wedding and spent hours gazing out at the sailboats on Lake Michigan. She'd bet not a single one of the occupants soaking up the warmth of the midday sun experienced one iota of the shame and disappointment she felt. By the time the sun started to set she still hadn't found the relief that she had made the right decision.

Raucous rock music drifted from the open doorway of the neighborhood tavern, snagging her attention. The only other sign of life in the older section of Chicago came from a closed market halfway down the block with a dim light spilling onto the pavement. She turned in the seat and looked behind her toward the market for a pay phone, seeing nothing more than a stretch of pavement and darkened storefronts. She couldn't very well sit in the car all night.

"Oh sweet Mary," she muttered. She was an adult. She had every right to walk into that bar and use the phone, and even order a drink if she wanted. So why was she hesitating?

She let out a sigh. Because twenty-four years of following rules told her a preacher's daughter didn't enter a bar without a male escort. Especially if the daughter in question was wearing a wedding gown!

With a lift of her chin and a determination to break her second rule in the same day, she scooped her little white satin bag from the passenger seat and climbed out of the car, thankfully without tripping over the voluminous yards of white satin.

She tugged hard on the train she hadn't had time to detach before her abrupt departure from her own wedding, ten feet of satin spilling from the driver's seat onto the asphalt. Not bothering with the elastic wristband, she bunched the fabric in her hand, slammed the door to her uncooperative Escort sedan, and walked resolutely toward the entrance below a green, flashing neon sign.

Blaring music and the stench of stale smoke and alcohol hit her when she slipped inside the bar. All she needed was a telephone to call a tow truck, and then she'd be on her way. Where, she hadn't decided, but she planned to stay as far away from Homer, Illinois, as possible.

She stepped up to the archway leading into the bar. Her confidence wavered. She could do this. How else was she going to learn to take care of herself, and more importantly, do things her way, if she couldn't even walk into a bar?

The song blasting from the jukebox at damaging decibel levels she recognized from an older MTV rock video. Flea. The lead singer's name was Flea, and in the video, most of his body had been covered in tattoos. Who would name their child Flea? she wondered.

Someone who ignored rules, that's who. Someone who grabbed life with both hands and shucked the restrictions of convention. Someone who didn't do everything that was expected of her without question. Someone who probably wouldn't feel half as awful as she did for running out on her own wedding.

A wooden sign above a long mirror covering the wall behind a mahogany bar caught her attention. For the first time in days, a genuine grin tugged her lips as she read the sign: Take a walk on The Wilde Side.

She couldn't think of anything more appropriate for a woman intent on breaking the rules.

THE WILDE SIDE was the last place Cooper Wilde expected to find a fairy princess, but damned if one hadn't just walked through the doors. A platinum blond fairy princess with a chickie-boom body and big, round turquoise eyes filled with apprehension. That intriguing gaze darted around the smoky bar before landing on him, sending awareness rumbling through him in Richter-scale-worthy shock waves.

She stood a little straighter and headed right for him as the Red Hot Chili Peppers segued into a classic rock standard by the Hollies. There was nothing long and cool about the hot little number dressed in bridal satin and lace, and Coop seriously doubted she'd ever stepped foot in a bar. Hell, he had suspicions about her even being of the legal age. He had enough trouble without getting busted with a minor in the bar.

She lifted her chin and ignored the stares of his few customers, a blue-collar crowd for the most part, their glances ranging from mild curiosity to a few outright leers that leapt straight across the border toward rude. She tightened her grip on a little satin bag clutched in her delicate fingers and stepped up to the long mahogany bar.

Coop crossed his arms and looked down at her, into those big eyes banked with a determination that filled him with dread. He had enough to worry about in what was becoming a vain attempt to keep the bar operational without having to deal with a jilted bride who didn't have the foresight to change clothes before traipsing around Chicago. His customers were mostly long-timers, harmless older guys he'd known practically his entire life, but there were a few rougher types who wouldn't hesitate to take advantage of a pretty little lady with busted dreams and a broken heart. As far as he was concerned, a lone woman in a wedding gown pretty much qualified under both categories.

The best thing he could do for The Wilde Side, and himself, was to send her back to fairyland as soon as possible. He didn't need to scan the pitifully thin crowd to know she was attracting a whole lot of attention. Attention that could get her into trouble.

"What can I do for you, Princess?"

"Do you have a pay phone?" she asked in a voice loud enough to be heard over the jukebox.

"In the back," he answered with a quick jerk of his head.

"Thank you," she answered primly.

He braced his hands on the bar and leaned forward.

"And you're in the wrong place, Princess. St. Mike's is a few blocks south of here." He pushed off the bar and strolled away, hoping she'd take the hint and leave.

"I'm looking for a telephone, not a church," she called after him.

He shrugged and opened the cooler for a fresh bottle of beer for Marty Davis, a welder who was his uncle's closest friend, and by extension, another surrogate father to Cooper. Hayden Wilde and Marty had been the ones to convince him eleven years ago, via ultimatum, to join the navy and see the world. He'd been a rebel of the first degree and intent on living up to his name. As much as he hadn't wanted to take their advice, the service had held a hell of a lot more appeal than jail, which was where he'd been heading fast.

He'd surprised not only himself, but his uncle as well, when he'd gone into SEAL training. The special forces team had intrigued him, and earning the nickname Wildman hadn't been too much of a stretch. He'd figured he'd do his four-year stint, but when the end of his term drew to a close, he'd gone to see the re-tention officer and reenlisted for another six years. He'd been about to re-up for another six when the chaplain had come to see him, telling him his uncle needed him to come home. Taking into consideration the heart attack Hayden had suffered the previous spring, Coop decided to come back to Chicago to take care of the man who'd raised him after his mother died.

What he found was not only Hayden in perfect health, but he'd let his life's work fall practically to ruin. And not because of any illness, as Coop had been led to believe. No, Hayden Wilde had been suffering from another unfortunate condition, one caused by faulty genetics. His obsession with the opposite sex had cost him more than his pride this time, it had almost cost him his business.

"And I want a drink," the princess yelled over the music in a voice filled with steely determination.

That got his attention and snapped him right back into the present. Coop set the beer in front of Marty, who didn't bother to hide his amusement, and moved back down the length of the bar toward her. "Not without some ID, Princess. I could lose my license for even allowing you in here."

She gave him a smug look and opened her little satin bag. "As you can see," she said, handing over her driver's license, "I'm well over the legal drinking age."

He took the ID from her. "Barely," he muttered, counting backward as he examined the small plastic card, alternately comparing the police lineup quality photo to the real thing. The real thing was much more interesting. Too bad he didn't have time for interesting, because Carly Cassidy was sassy and curvy. Throw in willing, and she'd be just the way he liked them, even if she was only three years above the legal drinking age.

Since he wasn't breaking the law by serving her, he handed the license back. "One drink, then you leave. I don't need your kind of trouble, Princess. What'll it be?"

Carly hadn't a clue. The only alcohol ever to pass her lips had been the sacramental kind. For her first drink, she wanted something interesting. One of those exotic kind the starlets in Hollywood sat around their swimming pools sipping, with colorful paper umbrellas and sweet tropical fruit perched on the side of the glass.

"We don't do frilly and frothy," the sexy bartender

said, practically reading her mind. He braced his hands on lean hips encased in soft, faded denim. "My customers like it hard and they like it fast."

She looked up at him, frowning when an odd tingling started to uncurl in her tummy. Hunger, she decided. Those strange tingles had nothing to do with the way the bartender's white T-shirt with an alcoholic beverage logo splashed across the front clung to the broadest shoulders and widest chest she'd ever had the privilege of viewing. Most assuredly hunger, she reminded herself, and not caused by the way his dark chocolate eyes swept over her or the way his mouth tipped up into a breathtaking grin that belied his surly attitude. She'd been so nervous she hadn't been able to eat breakfast, that's all. The huge feast at the wedding reception...well, she *had* missed that. Yes, she decided firmly. Most definitely hunger.

"Scotch," she finally blurted, wondering if she'd even like whiskey. Anything was better than another round of guilt. "On the rocks."

One of his rich sable eyebrows lifted. "One finger or two?"

Fingers? Was that bar slang for ice cubes?

She shrugged. "Two should be sufficient."

The gorgeous hunk of a bartender gave her a skeptical look, then moved down the bar to fix her drink.

Keeping her satin bag clutched firmly in her hand, she headed toward the rear of the tavern, passing between a pair of pool tables and a couple of rough-and-tumble-looking men with cue sticks in one hand and amber bottles of beer in the other. They looked at her curiously, and she couldn't exactly blame them. Odds were that not many women actually frequented The Wilde Side dressed in a wedding gown.

Nestled at the end of a short hallway next to the ladies' room, she found the pay phone with a tattered copy of the phone book attached to the wall by a metal cord. She made her call for the tow truck only to learn she'd be waiting for a minimum of two hours. It was, after all, Saturday night.

She hung up, deciding to wait for the tow truck driver to arrive before she called a taxi. She took a step to turn and ran smack into a brick wall of leather, denim and chains.

She looked up, tipping her head far back to stare into one of the most homely faces she'd ever had the misfortune of viewing. Biker Boy's eyes were beady and wide set, and focused on some point south of her face. His nose was crooked, obviously it'd been broken—more than once.

He grinned, revealing a missing front tooth. "'Scuse me, miss, but my buddy and me was wondering if them were real?"

Carly's jaw fell slack. Where she came from, strange men did not approach women and ask if their...*if their breasts were real!*

She snapped her mouth closed. She wasn't in Homer. No one here expected her to murmur a polite "excuse me" then quietly step around the gentleman, pretending he hadn't just insulted her. If she followed the rules as she'd done all her life, that's exactly what she would do in the face of such an impropriety.

Who was she kidding? If she'd followed the rules the way she was supposed to, she wouldn't even be having this conversation. She'd be spending her wedding night at the Village Inn in her hometown before setting off tomorrow for the Florida Keys with her groom.

Rules. She hated them, but worse, despised herself

for simply following along like a good little girl. Rules had nearly ruined her life. They'd almost seen her married to a man she didn't love and who didn't love her. Because of them, she'd accepted a position as a music teacher at her hometown high school, when that was the last thing she wanted to do for the rest of her life.

Well, Carly Cassidy was finished following rules!

"Actually," she said, flashing Biker Boy a blithe grin, "it's this damn corset I'm wearing. Ridiculous contraption, don't you think?"

Biker Boy's beady eyes rounded, making him look almost cross-eyed. His crooked nose turned bright pink, the color slowly spreading over his wide, puffy cheeks.

He cleared his throat. "I meant your eyes, miss. They're a real nice turquoise color, and Joe thought they was them colored contacts some women like."

"Oh." Heat spread over her own cheeks. "I'm so sorry. I thought...I thought you meant... Oh sweet Mary, she felt like a fool. Even if she was through following everyone else's rules, rudeness was quite unacceptable. She felt just awful for embarrassing him. Although she had to admit, Biker Boy and blushing weren't exactly synonymous.

His gap-toothed grin was sheepish. "It's okay. So are they? Your *eyes*," he added meaningfully.

She grinned for the second time that day. "Yes, they're real. And I really am sorry. Uh...can I buy you a drink? You know, as an apology."

Biker Boy took a step back and swept his beady blue gaze over her. "Don't you have someplace to go?"

"Not until the tow truck driver shows up for my car." Even then, she had no particular destination in mind, but she'd worry about that later. From now on, she was going to make her own rules. Carly's Law, she thought, with a mutinous lift of her chin, would be to live life as it comes, and do it with gusto. Provided she could shelve the guilt plaguing her, she might even be able to start living by her new laws. Once she decided what they were, of course.

She stooped to gather her dress, then smiled up at Biker Boy. "Do you have a name?" she asked. She didn't think he'd appreciate the nickname she'd given him, but the faded Harley-Davidson motorcycle T-shirt was rather telling.

"Benny," he said, flashing her a grin again.

"Well, Benny," she said, tossing the train over her arm. "I have a drink waiting for me at the bar, so unless you plan to join me, you'll have to excuse me."

She marched back inside the barroom and headed straight for the bar and the lone drink waiting for her on a paper napkin. With a little concentration and ingenuity, she managed to climb onto the bar stool despite the weight of her dress. She set her bag in front of her, reached for the glass and took her first very unladylike drink of straight Scotch.

The fiery brew instantly seared her throat. Her stomach roiled, then ignited into a ball of flame. What had the bartender given her? Lighter fluid?

She coughed, sputtered, then wheezed out a breath. Undaunted, she downed another fraction of whiskey. The second drink felt no better than the first.

Benny and his friend approached her, occupying a bar stool on either side of her. "This is Joe." Benny introduced his friend with a crook of his thumb. "He thought your eyes were fake."

Carly looked over at Joe. He wasn't quite as homely

as Benny, but someone needed to have a serious discussion with him about personal hygiene.

"Are you a mechanic by any chance?" she asked, wondering how anyone could have that much grease under his fingernails and not spend his day beneath the hood of someone's car.

Joe grinned. Joe had all of his teeth, she noticed. "I fix lawn mowers."

Carly nodded, then took another drink of whiskey. Too bad, she thought. Maybe she could've gotten him to take a look at her car and figure out why it had died.

By her fourth attempt at the Scotch, she'd started to feel just a teensy bit numb. Numb was good. Numb didn't allow room for guilt or regrets.

Someone fired up the jukebox again, and a series of alarms sounded, followed by the mellow strum of an electric guitar. Benny signaled for the bartender, who took his sweet time. "What'll it be boys?" she asked them, flashing Mr. Tall, Dark and Handsome a grin that only made his frown deepen.

"I thought I told you one drink," he said, his voice a heck of lot smoother than the alcohol he served. He flipped the cap off two bottles of beer and set them in front of Benny and Joe.

"Give her a break, Wilde," Joe said. "She's waiting for a tow truck."

Wilde looked at her with hard eyes. "She doesn't belong here."

"*She* has a name," Carly said before draining her glass. "And it's Carly. And Carly wants another—" she pointed at her empty glass, trying like the devil to remember what she'd just ordered "—another one of these."

Those dark chocolate eyes narrowed, but she ignored that and concentrated on his face. He has a nice chin, she thought. Strong and square. And those eyes. A soft sigh escaped her lips. A woman could easily get lost in all that intensity.

A series of little tingles skirted along her spine, then spread outward over her tummy, making her feel warm and cozy. If this was the way alcohol made people feel, no wonder such a large majority of the population imbibed on occasion.

Wilde braced his hands on the bar and leaned forward. She watched in fascination as his biceps strained against the fabric of his white T-shirt. The urge to trace her fingers along all that muscle was strong. Too strong, she thought, and frowned. Funny, but she'd never once considered doing that to her abandoned bridegroom.

"Don't you have someplace else to go?" he asked, his deep voice as intoxicating as his eyes, no matter how disagreeable his attitude. Well, not exactly disagreeable, she amended, but he wasn't the most friendly person she'd ever met.

She let out another little sigh and propped her chin in her hand and looked into eyes filled with distrust. "Not for the moment."

"Isn't someone wondering where you are?" he asked, looking pointedly at her wedding dress.

She ignored the reminder of her current state of shame and traced her finger along the rim of her empty glass, still wishing she could do the same to those incredible biceps and corded forearms.

"Oh, I'm sure they're all quite curious." Curious, concerned and disappointed in her. She'd never done anything remotely irresponsible in her life...until now.

The Rolling Stones began singing for a little sympathy for the devil. "Don't you have any music from *this* century on that jukebox?" she asked him, anxious to change the subject. She didn't want to start thinking about what she'd done or about the people she'd hurt by running off like a big fat coward.

"You want Top Forty, Princess, you'll have to go to City Lights." He slapped a damp towel on the bar in front of her. "I'd be more than happy to call you a cab."

She ignored his blatant hint to leave and turned her head to the side, resting her temple against her fist. She let her gaze wander over the dozen or so patrons in The Wilde Side before looking back at Wilde. "I bet if you smiled more, you'd attract a lot more customers."

He pushed off the bar, taking his damp rag with him, but not before giving her a look that said he didn't appreciate her free public relations consultation. When he returned, he set the drink in front of her, and shot Benny and Joe a warning look before moving down the bar a few paces.

A warning about what? she wanted to know.

Benny leaned forward, bracing his big beefy elbows on the bar. "You from around here, Carly?"

She took a sip of her Scotch, keeping her gaze on Wilde. Using long, slender fingers, he gathered empty glasses from the bar and set them in a tub of soapy water. He turned, and she caught a glimpse of his backside, admiring the way the soft denim hugged his body. The man definitely wore his jeans well.

She looked at Benny. "I'm sorry, did you say something?"

"Are you from around here?"

She shook her head. "Nope."

"Just passing through?" Joe asked before lifting the bottle to his lips.

She frowned and thought for a minute before nodding slowly. "That about sums it up," she said quietly.

Benny turned, leaning on the bar, and looked down at her. "So, uh...where's your groom?"

"I don't know," she said around the sudden tightness in her throat. "He's probably being consoled by our families and friends because of what I did."

Carly's frown deepened. Because she'd panicked, she'd hurt people, and that bothered her more than her uncertain future. Family was still important to her, and heaven knew she had more than her share of family to go around. She'd been selfish and irresponsible, and the guilt weighed heavily upon her shoulders.

How was she going to break rules if she couldn't do it without harboring guilt?

She sucked in a deep, shuddering breath and looked up at Benny. And then she burst into tears.

2

Rule 2: A lady will always strive to maintain a hint of mystery.

COOP SLID A pilsner glass over the scrub brush inside the metal tub of hot soapy water. He concentrated on twisting the glass over the scrub instead of allowing his gaze to drift back to the platinum bride with the chickie-boom curves and eyes the color of the Mediterranean Sea at sunset.

She was trouble. The kind of trouble a guy like him enjoyed and could easily be attracted to if he'd let himself get involved.

He couldn't afford to get involved, not when he had a business to salvage.

He swished the glass a few more times over the scrub before dipping it into the tub of clear hot water, then added it to the rack to dry. The Stones CD on the jukebox faded into Carlos Santana's sultry ode to a black magic woman, the momentary silence between CDs interrupted by hushed conversation and a sudden wail from the south end of the bar.

Cooper let out a sigh and shook his head, fighting the urge to stop what he was doing and head back down the bar toward the lush little number in white. That plaintive wail of hers was easily a barometer to her sorry emotional state, which no doubt included equal doses of regret and guilt now that a couple of stiff drinks had dulled the shock of her act of desperation.

Benny looked helplessly at his buddy Joe. "Don't cry, Carly. I didn't mean to upset you."

Carly muttered something Coop couldn't quite make out, then she looked up at Benny. After a rather noisy sniffle, she dropped her forehead against the bar and sobbed louder.

Coop hid the wry grin on his lips when Benny's jaw fell slack. "It'll be okay," Benny said, thumping the crying woman on the back in a rough attempt at sympathy.

"You gonna do something 'bout that, Coop?" Marty hitched his thumb in the blubbering bride's direction. "She's gonna chase off the customers, son, and you can't afford that. If we wanted to hear a woman whine, we'd stay home."

Considering his blue-collar clientele, Marty definitely had a point, Cooper thought. Fred and Lou were already loading their custom pool cues into their cases and preparing to leave.

"Why me?" Cooper muttered. He slapped a dry towel over his shoulder. "Of all the bars in Chicago, why this one?"

Marty chuckled. "Face it, Coop. When it comes to luck, if it wasn't for bad, you wouldn't have any."

He very nearly agreed, except the pitiful state of The Wilde Side wasn't of his making. No, that had been Hayden's doing, or undoing, he thought grumpily. He'd known exactly what he was getting into when he'd promised his uncle he'd take care of the place—a lost cause. The neighborhood tavern had been around since the late fifties, and a few of the regulars never failed to remind him that the bar was as much a part of Chicago history as old Mrs. Leary's cow. He could probably teach the teary bride a few things about guilt, he thought, because every time he considered closing down the bar, that's exactly what he felt—a hefty dose of guilt about going back on a promise to his uncle.

Luck had nothing to do with the obstacles Coop faced. Poor planning and allowing a woman to cloud his uncle's judgment did, however, and Coop had nothing to blame but his loyalty to Hayden for his current problems and the sorry state of his own finances. He couldn't afford to dump another dime into the bar, but if things didn't turn around soon, he'd have no choice but to close the doors for good. And a blubbering bride chasing off what customers he had left wasn't helping matters.

He headed down the bar toward the odd threesome, stopping long enough to lower the volume on the jukebox. Benny and Joe were good guys, rough on the outside and always anxious for a little action, legal or otherwise. But anyone who took the time to get to know Benny West or Joe Lanford knew they were a couple of pussycats underneath the scruffy denim and chrome chains. What did surprise Cooper, though, was their matching soft spots for the curvy little damsel in distress. They made a habit of steering clear of the sweet and pure types, not that any frequented the bar, but one look at the teary bride and Cooper knew she'd easily reside at the top of the good-girl list.

Oh well, he thought, snagging a box of tissues from behind the bar. At least with Benny and Joe playing bodyguard, not many would be anxious to hassle the bride.

He slapped the box of tissues down in front of her.

"Turn off the waterworks, Princess. You're spooking my customers."

She sniffed and lifted her short cap of platinum curls, casting those intriguing eyes filled with moisture his way. Something twisted behind his ribs at the despondency cloaked in her gaze. Certainly not his heart. He didn't need this. Not now when he was a bank statement away from financial ruin. Hadn't he learned anything from the mistakes of his uncle and his mother?

Obviously not, considering the way the buxom bride was making his heart slam into his ribs every time she shifted her turquoise eyes in his direction.

"I'm sor...sorry," she said, a huge tear spilling from her spiked lashes. "I'm not supposed to cry in public."

"Who said you can't cry in public?" Joe asked, his gravelly voice filled with genuine sympathy as he gently patted her shoulder.

Another sniff followed a tug on a tissue from the box. She looked at Joe. "It's a rule."

"Who made up a dumb rule like that?" Benny asked, his puffy face filled with curiosity.

Carly shrugged, a barely perceptible lift of one satin-clad shoulder that drew Coop's gaze like a magnet to a pair of very full breasts. "I don't know," she said, dabbing her eyes. "But there are thousands of them. And I've always adhered to them, until now."

Coop crossed his arms over his chest and rocked back on his heels. "What do your rules say about a bride in a bar without her groom?"

Carly pulled in a deep breath.

Cooper winced and waited, wishing he'd kept to the opposite end of the bar.

She wailed again, burying her face in the already crumpled tissue.

"Aw, Coop. Now look what you did," Benny chided him. He smacked Carly on the back with his beefy hand in another poor gesture of comfort.

"Ow," she muttered between sobs.

"We just got her calmed down," Joe said, shooting him a disgruntled glance. "Why'd you have to go and get her started up again?"

Coop gave them both a hard look. "Why don't you two find out where she belongs and see about returning her?"

"She's not a lost puppy," Benny scolded. His pencil-thin eyebrows pinched together in a frown. "Some guy stood her up. On her wedding day."

Carly shook her head, blond curls bouncing with the movement. "No, he didn't." She reached for another tissue. "I...I ran away," she managed before issuing another ear-splitting wail.

Cooper rolled his eyes. He tried to tell himself he didn't care. He didn't care about her or why she'd left her groom at the altar. The firm reprimand didn't change the fact that he was lying to himself, nor lessen the gnawing in his gut he could only describe as something a lot more interesting than curiosity.

Something he didn't want or need. Dammit, he'd made a promise and he wasn't about to let a voluptuous female, no matter how attractive, distract him. And Carly had diversion written all over her.

"Just keep it down," he groused, then moved a couple of feet down the bar to serve another customer.

"I'm sure you had a very good reason for leaving like that," Joe said, sliding her drink closer. "Here. Drink up, Carly. It'll cure what ails ya."

She dropped the bunched-up tissues on the bar and took the glass in both hands, downing the Scotch as if it was no stronger than a soft drink. Cooper didn't want to be around when all that booze hit.

She hiccuped and waved her slender hand in the air. "Could I have another, please?"

"Anything you want, Carly," Joe said, his gruff voice ridiculously saccharine. "You just tell Joe all about it, okay?"

"Aw, hell," Cooper muttered to himself. If she wanted to get plastered, then that was her problem. What did he care if she'd have the devil to pay come morning when she woke up with a whopper of a hangover? It wasn't as if *he'd* be holding her head while she bowed to the porcelain god.

He delivered another Scotch, adding more water than booze to her glass, then moved down the bar to take care of a few more customers before wandering back toward her and her mismatched caretakers.

Curiosity, he told himself. That's the only reason he continued to take up residence at the south end of the bar. He was curious as to how she came to be in his tavern. It had nothing whatsoever to do with attraction, sexual or otherwise, even if he couldn't seem to keep his gaze from straying to those lush curves.

She looked at him when he stopped in front of her, and his gut tightened.

Damn!

Curiosity, he attempted to convince himself again. He was *not* reacting to those big turquoise eyes.

She braced her elbows on the bar and hung her head, her soft white-blond curls swaying forward, brushing her cheeks. Hunched slightly over the bar like a regular, she provided him with a perfect view of her ample cleavage. Damned if he could drag his eyes away to safer territory. If he wasn't careful, he'd start drooling any minute.

Images filtered through his mind.

Erotic images.

Cooper frowned. He didn't have time for this, no matter how tempting or alluring.

"I tried to tell him yesterday," she said suddenly.

"Who?" Joe asked, tipping back his beer.

"Dean," she said, trailing her finger over the rim of her glass. "I tried to tell him when we went to meet my sisters at the country club to finish the decorations for the reception. I tried to tell him and he just wouldn't listen to me."

Benny shrugged. "Hey, at least you tried," he added sympathetically.

"There are over three hundred family and friends eating chicken Kiev right now. Baked potatoes with little pats of butter molded into perfect squares with my and Dean's initials on them. They were supposed to be celebrating the beginning of our life together."

She reached for the glass and tossed the contents back like a shot. "He just wouldn't listen," she said again. "He kept insisting it was only prewedding jitters."

Considering she was on her third drink, she hadn't slurred a single word despite Coop's doubts about her being an experienced drinker. Her skin looked too soft and smooth, having none of the telltale signs of someone who frequented the bottom of a bottle. His fingers itched to touch her, to see for himself if her skin was as silky as it looked.

He made a fist and turned away, moving down the bar to serve a couple of men he didn't recognize.

They'd come into The Wilde Side looking for a little re-laxation, or a little action. From the sly glances they cast in Carly's direction, Cooper had a bad feeling ac-tion would be on the menu for the night, unless he found a way to get rid of her.

For the next hour, he served customers, refilled drinks and made polite conversation. A few of the guys asked him about the lone bride, but for the most part, other than an occasional off-color joke, now that she'd finally quieted, no one paid her much attention.

During a brief lull, and against his better judgment, he found an excuse to wander down to her end of the bar again.

Benny polished off his beer and requested another. "I almost got married once," Cooper heard him tell Carly.

Her head snapped around and she blinked a few times. "You did?"

Cooper slid a fresh beer in front of Benny, hiding his grin at her reaction. When a guy was as butt-ugly as Benny West, chasing women didn't exactly mean he'd catch them.

"Sure did," Benny said, a hint of melancholy in his voice. "But I didn't like the thought of being tied down to one woman."

Carly blinked several times, but Cooper had to give her credit when she kept a straight face. Either she was already ripped or one of the most tenderhearted crea-tures he'd ever met.

"Did your limbs quake?" she asked.

"Naw," Benny said, flashing her that gap-toothed grin. "But I puked once."

Carly's jaw dropped. "Really?"

Cooper cleared his throat to keep from laughing, then grabbed a damp rag to start wiping down the bar.

At Benny's nod, she turned her attention to Joe. "Are you married?"

Joe set his beer aside. "Not me. No way."

She tilted her head to the side, those bouncy curls brushing her cheek. "I don't think marriage is all bad," she said after a moment. "Not really. I've got six older sisters, and they're all happily married. Well, not Jill," she said, as if they knew to whom she was referring. "But that'll probably change soon."

"Maybe you weren't ready to get married," Cooper reasoned, wanting to bite his tongue off for getting involved. Would he ever learn?

Carly flashed her intriguing gaze his way. "Probably not," she said quietly. A frown tugged her brows together. "But how do you know when you're ready?"

Cooper didn't answer, because he didn't know what to say that wouldn't shatter those little-girl illusions she no doubt harbored. When it came to marriage, role models had been in short supply for him. From the few guys he'd known in the navy who'd walked down the aisle, he'd learned that marriage and the navy didn't mix. As a SEAL, he hadn't spent much time in one place and had wisely chosen not to tie himself down. Even with the lack of role models in his life, he knew wedded bliss wouldn't be a reality unless he came home more than a couple of days every month or two.

When he didn't provide a response, Carly looked to Benny and Joe for insight. Both men remained silent, contemplating their beers. "That's what I thought," she said after a few moments.

Benny turned and gave her a wide grin. "You know what you need?"

Carly let out a hefty sigh, crossed her arms on the bar and rested her cheek on her satin-covered forearms. "Sure. A job, a place to live and some serious direction in my life."

Benny shook his head. "Uh-uh. You need to have some fun and just forget about everything else for a while."

"Great idea," Joe added.

She lifted her head to look at Benny. "How long is a while?"

Benny shrugged. "I dunno. Tonight. A week. A month."

Joe slapped his hand on the bar. "How about a year?"

She straightened, her eyes filling with interest. Dangerous interest, in Cooper's opinion.

"You're suggesting I just run away from my problems?"

Cooper scooped her empty glass off the bar. "Isn't that why you're here?" he asked.

She turned her head, her gaze colliding with his. "That wasn't very nice."

He shrugged. "I just call 'em as I see 'em, Princess."

Her chin lifted a notch and a defiant light sparked in her gaze, highlighting her irises with tiny flecks of gold. Why that made his gut tighten even more, he couldn't be sure, but he sure as hell liked the way she looked at him. She might be an emotional wreck, but he suspected there was too much fire and spunk behind the teary-eyed bride routine for her bout of alcohol-enriched depression to last for very long.

And damn if he didn't like fire and spunk.

A lot.

She made a noise that bordered on a snort, then

turned her attention back to her bodyguards. That chin of hers inched upward another defiant notch, too. "What kind of fun?" she asked, determination lacing her sweet voice.

The big guy shrugged. "Wanna shoot some pool?"

She glanced over her shoulder to the pool tables. "I don't know how to play."

"It's okay," Joe said, standing. "We'll teach you."

She shrugged and slid off the bar stool. "Okay. But only until the tow truck driver shows up. Then I have to leave."

And go where? Cooper almost asked, but stopped himself in time. He didn't care. He didn't want to care, but there was something about her that spiked his interest, regardless of what a distraction like her could cost him.

"Let's make it interesting," Joe suggested, leading her away from the bar. "Let's play for drinks. Winner buys."

Lyrical laughter drifted to Cooper as he kept a watchful eye on the bride while pulling a beer from the cooler. For the next hour or two, other than an occasional glance in her direction, he didn't have time to worry about Carly. She was safe with Benny and Joe. It was Saturday night, and thankfully the bar was somewhat busy for a change. With his waitress off because of a sick kid, he was on his own, and he didn't have time to baby-sit a hot number in white, even if his gaze kept straying toward her more times than he cared to admit.

By midnight, the bride had disappeared without a word, and he tried to tell himself what he felt wasn't even remotely close to disappointment, but gratitude. The last thing he needed was to get tangled up with a woman when he had more important things to worry about. Like finding a way to hang on to The Wilde Side until his uncle came to his senses again.

By the time he ushered the last customer from the bar, Coop was beat. He emptied the till and started cleaning up rather than putting it off until the next day. Sunday was the only day of the week the bar opened later in the afternoon, and he looked forward to a few extra hours to himself.

As he mopped the floors, his mind drifted to the platinum blonde with the lush body. While he finished cleaning up the men's room, he wondered if perhaps he should've asked her two self-appointed bodyguards where she'd gone.

She was none of his business, he thought grumpily, flipping off the light. He shoved the mop into the metal bucket and wheeled it across the hall to the ladies' room. It wasn't as if he'd ever see her again. Or even that he cared.

Then why couldn't he stop thinking about her, wondering if she was all right?

Because he was genetically predisposed. How could he stop thinking about her when his DNA forbade it? He couldn't, and gave a heartfelt thanks to his guardian angel for taking the Princess out of the equation.

He pushed open the door to the ladies' room. Miles of dirty white satin spilled from beneath the door of the last stall, tangled around a delicately shaped foot.

Cooper swore colorfully. So much for someone upstairs looking out for him.

"Party's over, Princess," he called out as he crossed the asphalt tiles to the last stall.

She didn't respond.

He pounded on the metal door. "You all right?"

No answer.

Great. Just what he didn't need. He let out a rough sigh followed by a few more curses and tried the door, but she'd locked it. This wasn't the first time some drunk had passed out in one of his bathrooms. But she wasn't some drunk, he reminded himself. She was a runaway bride who'd had too much to drink after an emotionally exhausting day, and no doubt on an empty stomach.

He had two choices, and neither option thrilled him. If he called Chicago's finest and let them deal with her, they'd toss her delectable backside behind bars. Having spent a few nights of his own in the drunk tank after carousing with his buddies on shore leave, the thought of her spending the night in one left him with a bad taste in his mouth. The other option left him with a sick feeling in the pit of his stomach.

He *had* no other option, he thought, at least none that would allow him to continue to live in peace with his conscience.

Crouching, he peered under the door. She was sound asleep, curled on her side, using her upper arm for a pillow. He slid his fingers over her slender ankle, ignoring the strong urge to smooth his hand over the rest of her shapely leg.

He tried to shake her awake. "Carly? Come on, Princess. Time to rise and shine," he said gently.

Nothing. Not even a soft little moan or a flutter of those lashes fanning her pale cheeks. She was out cold.

"So much for not being around when the booze hit," he complained, then worked to open the stall. Once he had it opened, he moved into the cramped space beside her, trying one last, useless time to wake her.

Carefully, he eased his arms around her and managed to get her and her cumbersome dress out of the stall. She issued a soft little moan when he lifted her into his arms, curling her slender hand against his chest. With the lightweight bundle held securely, he concentrated on getting her upstairs into his apartment without tripping over her dress, and not the way her full breasts brushed against his chest when she sleepily wound her arms around his neck.

He shouldered his way down a short hallway to his old bedroom. "Enjoy it while it lasts, Princess," he said, easing her onto the twin mattress. "In a few hours, you're gonna be feeling like you've been run down by a Peterbilt truck at full speed."

He straightened and looked down at her, not sure what to do next. There were still things in the bar that needed his attention, but he couldn't very well leave her trussed up in her wedding dress and Lord knew what else for the night. Or could he?

No, he decided against his better judgment. He couldn't, but the thought of removing all that satin to reveal smooth skin didn't exactly appeal to him, either. He took that back. It more than appealed to him, and that was the first and foremost reason for him to walk out and leave her be, regardless of how uncomfortable she looked.

Muttering a few more curses, he started with her shoes, then pushed up the heavy satin to reveal the lacy tops of white stockings covering the shapeliest pair of legs he'd ever seen.

He eased out a breath. *Very nice.*

What the hell was wrong with him? As if he didn't have enough trouble, here he was borrowing more than he could handle by undressing a woman—an unconscious woman—he didn't even know. Convinced he was certifiable and just looking to get his butt sued, or worse, he removed her stockings anyway, along with a blue satin and lace garter her groom should have slid from her leg as dictated by tradition.

She sighed, a soft sound that stirred his blood. Ignoring the heat uncurling in his belly, he tugged the satin down to cover her legs, then shifted her weight to expose a long row of pearl buttons running along her spine. Once he had them undone, he eased the dress from her arms and managed to pull the heavy fabric away from her.

Cooper was sweating, and it had nothing to do with the warmth of the sultry evening and everything to do with the beauty lying in his childhood bed with her legs angled in a seductive pose. Wearing a scant pair of pure white lace panties cut high on her thigh and a matching corset that enhanced the swell of her breasts, she was a vision.

A sensual vision that had his blood pumping fast through his veins.

And a distraction he didn't need or welcome.

He left the bedroom only to return a few minutes later with one of his T-shirts. Lifting her in his arms again, he pulled the shirt over her head and slipped her limp arms through the sleeves. Once he had her decently covered, he worked the back lacing of the corset, pulled it from around her and firmly tugged the shirt down.

A dreamy little sigh escaped her parted lips when he eased her back onto the bed. "Hmm," she murmured, turning onto her side. Her hand landed in his lap, dangerously close to his fly.

Her slender fingers flexed.

A flash of heat flared in his gut and spread south.

He sat on the edge of the bed staring down at her, his gaze divided between the blissful expression on her face and the delicate fingers brushing his fly.

What the hell was he supposed to do with her now?

Absolutely nothing!

He had a business to salvage thanks to Hayden's obsession with the opposite sex. He couldn't afford a distraction, especially one with a body made for sin and a sassy glint in her turquoise gaze capable of sending his testosterone levels soaring.

"Nothing," he muttered, and gently eased away from her.

He crossed the room and flipped off the overhead light, quietly closing the door behind him. He hoped his lapse into knight in shining armor was brief, praying it wouldn't cost him any more than it already had: the unexpected need clawing his gut.

Too bad the only relief he suspected existed resided in the form of a buxom Princess sleeping off the effects of too much alcohol on an empty stomach.

3

Rule 3: A lady will never openly seek an invitation, but will wait until one has been extended to her.

CONSCIOUSNESS returned with a vengeance.

Carly eased her eyes open to mere slits, then quickly squeezed them closed against the blinding sunlight streaming through an open window. A series of jackhammers pounded on the street, or somewhere.

Her head?

Sweet Mary, what had she done?

Like a bad movie, the events of the previous day swam through her muddled and pounding head. Her panicked flee from the church. A hastily written note with virtually no explanation as to why she couldn't go through with the wedding. The drive into Chicago. Her car breaking down in front of a bar, followed by far too many Scotch on the rocks for someone who'd never tasted anything stronger than sacramental wine.

She opened her eyes and groaned, grabbing her head in both hands, hoping to still the memories and lessen the pounding. She failed on both counts.

A flash of color caught her attention. Carefully, she opened one eye. Blue. Navy blue cotton?

She sat up quickly—too quickly—and heard the sound of a pitiful moan. Good grief, was that her?

One hand continued to hold on to her head, while

the other shot to her rolling stomach. A few deep breaths later, she eased her eyes open again and looked down.

She was wearing a T-shirt.

A man's T-shirt?

Frowning took too much energy, so she simply looked around the unfamiliar room. Where was she? Nothing snagged a memory. Worse, there just weren't any memories, no clues as to how she ended up in a strange room dressed in a man's T-shirt.

She spied her wedding gown laid carefully over a wooden ladder-back chair in front of an old student desk and gasped. Not only her wedding gown but her stockings, garter and corset, as well, all neatly folded and sitting on the corner of the desk. Had someone undressed her? Had she...?

"Oh, sweet Mary."

Carefully, she eased her legs over the side of the twin bed and stood, the hem of the T-shirt reaching a few inches above her knees. Thankfully, the room didn't spin. She vaguely recalled spinning, but not here, not in this room. It had been somewhere cool that smelled of bleach and disinfectant.

She shook her head, then groaned when a fresh flash of pain stabbed behind her light-sensitive eyes. She crossed an old braided rug to the door, then quietly stepped into a short hallway. The dulled hardwood floor was cool beneath her feet as she debated heading down the corridor toward the intoxicating aroma of fresh-brewed coffee or making use of the bathroom directly across the hall.

The bathroom won.

She took care of her immediate needs, then splashed cool water on her face. Studiously avoiding her reflection in the mirror, she opened the medicine chest in search of toothpaste. A tube with the cap snapped firmly in place sat on the lower shelf beside a single toothbrush, a container of floss and a bottle of inexpensive aftershave. Whomever had taken her home was neat, and single.

Since her own toothbrush and other toiletries were still in her car in the overnight bag she'd snagged before bolting from Homer, she made use of her unknown host's toothpaste by spreading it on the tip of her finger. She snapped the medicine chest closed, then further invaded his privacy by liberating a comb and attempting to restore a bit of semblance to her hair.

Feeling about as refreshed as she could without the benefit of a hot shower and a change of clothes, she left the sanctity of the small tiled bathroom and slowly made her way down the corridor. To her immediate left, a door stood open. Ignoring everything she'd ever been taught about good manners, she peered inside, hoping to gain any amount of knowledge possible about the identity of her host. All she received was further confirmation of his cleanliness, which pretty much eliminated Benny or Joe, based solely on their scruffy attire.

Still clueless, she left the corridor and entered a comfortably and neatly furnished living room. No newspapers cluttered the old but shining surface of a square coffee table. Not a single magazine lay near the vinyl recliner or was tossed carelessly on the shelf of the wall unit, which doubled as an entertainment center and bookshelf. Even the CDs and videocassettes were arranged in neat rows and—she peered closer—in alphabetical order. The only occupant in the wood-paneled living room was an overweight white cat, stretched over the back of the sofa. His big, round green eyes shot her a look of disdain before the furry beast hopped off his perch and meowed his way into another room.

Hoping the cat would offer some sort of clue as to her whereabouts, she followed. She stilled at the sound of a deep, masculine voice chastising the cat affectionately.

She knew that voice from somewhere.

Before she had time to resurrect the memory, the owner of the voice, followed by the cat, rounded the corner and stopped. Carly stared at a wide chest. Her gaze dipped to faded denim hugging lean hips and long legs, to bare feet. She didn't need him to turn around to know his backside was one incredible specimen of masculine perfection. She'd spent enough time last night admiring that view.

Dragging her gaze away from all that perfection, she tipped her head back and looked into eyes the color of dark chocolate. She stifled a groan. Of all the people in Chicago, she had to end up half-naked in the grumpy bar owner's apartment.

Had *he* undressed her? Just the thought of those hands on her body, her unconscious body, made her skin heat.

The missing pieces of her memory fell rapidly into place, particularly how rudely she'd behaved to him. Even telling herself he deserved it considering he'd been equally rude, not to mention judgmental, did nothing to lessen her embarrassment.

Not knowing what else to do, she extended her hand. "How do you do," she said, pushing her hair out of her eyes with her left hand. "I'm Carly Cassidy, and

I don't think I've ever been more embarrassed in my life."

She wished he would at least smile. She vaguely remembered his was one of those breath-stealing types. Sweet and sexy enough to make her heart flutter in her chest. Unfortunately, he wasn't in a smiling mood this morning. He just looked down at her with that intense gaze as if deciding what to do with her.

"Considering your life only consists of twenty-four years, that's not saying much." He shifted his coffee mug to his left hand, then grasped hers in a firm grip that sent a series of tingles shooting up her arm to settle in the tips of her breasts.

"Cooper Wilde."

She slowly pulled her hand from his. The tingling didn't stop. "I don't know whether to say it's been a pleasure or not."

A half grin lifted one corner of his mouth. "No, I don't suppose you would. Coffee?"

"Any chance you might have some tea handy?" she asked, telling herself she was *not* affected by his lopsided grin. She'd heard him laugh the night before and seemed to remember the sound had made her feel all warm and fuzzy inside. He really was quite attractive, frowns and all. If a girl went for all those angled lines and rough edges.

He shot her a look that said I think not.

"Coffee works for me."

She followed him into a small, compact kitchen, tugging on the hem of the T-shirt. He pulled a mug from the cabinet and filled it. "Black?"

Why not? she thought, and nodded. After what she'd consumed previously, black coffee would be a definite improvement.

"I don't mean to be rude," she said, taking the mug from him before following him out of the room to a small square dining table beneath a pair of windows. "But, exactly where am I and how did I get here?"

He sat in a chair and leaned back. "I found you passed out in the ladies' room after closing."

She set her mug on the table and dropped into another vinyl padded chair. "Oh sweet Mary," she muttered, dropping her head into her hands. Now she knew what had been cool and smelled of bleach and disinfectant. The bathroom floor!

He lifted his mug to his lips, his bittersweet gaze regarding her over the rim, revealing nothing other than perhaps mild interest. "It was either bring you up here or call the cops."

"Thank you." She could just imagine what her family would have to say about a visit on the wrong side of the divider at the local Gray Bar Hotel. *Hi Dad, it's Carly. Just calling you from my jail cell to tell you I'm fine.*

She frowned and looked over at Cooper. "'Up here?'" she asked, taking a sip of much-needed caffeine. The cat purred and dropped onto his side, stretching his large furry body beneath a sunbeam streaming through the open window.

"I live above the bar," Cooper said.

Made sense, she thought. It was convenient. That thought made her frown deepen, wondering if he often brought home stray women. No, she decided. The single toothbrush told the truth. Cooper Wilde was extremely single and excessively neat. Even his hair was neat, cut in a short cropped style. No stray locks of sable brushing that forehead. Everything had a place and everything was in its place. No doubt he viewed her as a disruption to his neat and orderly lifestyle.

Well, now what was she going to do? She had no clothes since they were locked in her car, and she couldn't very well prance around the city of Chicago in his T-shirt or her filthy wedding gown looking for a place to live.

Her car!

"Did the tow truck ever show up last night?" she asked him.

He turned to look out the window. "Either that or your car's been stolen."

"My purse. Do you have my purse?" If the driver had shown up, he would have given her a business card, or had her sign a receipt of some sort. Something to tell her the whereabouts of her vehicle, a change of clothes and her own toothbrush.

He stood and walked across the small dining area to a built-in cabinet. Opening a long center drawer, he pulled out her satin bag. "I found it when I went back down to finish closing the bar last night. You're lucky it was there."

She ignored the censure in his voice and opened the purse to riffle through the meager contents. Everything was there, except two twenties, which she'd no doubt spent last night in the bar. Unfortunately, no business card or receipt from the tow company. "Do you have a phone book?" she asked before he sat.

He retrieved the phone book and a cordless phone and set them in front of her, then disappeared into the kitchen. The cat promptly followed.

She scanned the pages until she found the name of the first tow company that sounded familiar. After a quick call to the dispatcher, she learned her car had indeed been towed to a local Ford dealership. The subsequent call was useless, however, since it was Sunday and the dealership was closed.

"You want to call someone to pick you up?" He placed a small plate with dry toast in front of her, and sat. Obviously he'd had experience with hangover remedies.

"Thank you," she said, and nibbled on the toast. She could call any one of her sisters and they'd come to her rescue as quickly as humanly possible. She could even call her parents. Except Carly was tired of being rescued. And she was fed up with doing what everyone always expected of her.

As the youngest daughter, she'd been expected to stay close to home. She'd been expected to finish college and return to the family fold. She'd done that.

Everyone expected her to teach at the local high school, just like her older sister Wendy. She'd accepted a position. As expected.

Everyone—her family, friends, and the majority of the population of Homer, Illinois—had expected her to marry Dean Langley, the only guy she'd ever dated. They started going out in high school, so of course everyone just assumed they'd marry when they continued their courtship through her years at college. She'd even agreed, as expected, she thought with a hefty dose of cynicism, but as the wedding drew closer, she knew she couldn't go through with it for one very simple reason—they weren't in love.

The day before the wedding, she'd asked Dean if he was in love with her. His response hadn't broken her heart, but had merely made her face the truth they'd both managed to avoid for months. Too many people had worked hard to make the wedding happen. Did she really want to disappoint them?

That was no reason to get married, as far as she was concerned, but Dean had countered her arguments with a diagnosis of prenuptial anxiety.

Anxiety about spending the rest of her life with a man she loved, rather than one she was *in love* with, she couldn't argue.

Yesterday she'd taken the first step. A faulty one, considering she'd given in to her case of cold feet, ended up in a bar, passed out and woke up in the apartment of a strange but very sexy man with warm brown eyes and a body she couldn't ignore without being a discredit to her gender.

She couldn't go back. If she did, she'd no doubt end up married to a man she didn't love, working in a job she didn't want and living the rest of her life wondering *what if.*

She shifted her gaze back to Cooper. "There's no one."

He leaned forward and braced his tanned forearms on the table. "I probably shouldn't bother, but considering you passed out in my bar *and* slept in my bed, I think that gives me some small right to ask.... Where are you from, Princess?"

Carly considered lying, but even if she was tired of following everyone else's rules, she couldn't forget twenty-four years of training and teaching by her minister father. Lying was one of *the* Top Ten, after all. "A small town about a hundred or so miles from here."

"Family?"

She smiled. "Do six older sisters, five brothers-in-law, both parents, three grandparents and a great-grandmother count? Oh, and a couple of aunts, uncles and innumerable cousins, too."

He leaned back in the chair and crossed his arms

over his chest. "Go home, Princess," he said gently. "You've got a lot of people who're probably worried about you."

She didn't doubt that for a minute, considering how she'd left without anything more than a note that said she was fine but couldn't go through with the wedding.

But how could she go home? She couldn't. Not with the rest of her life at stake.

She looked across the table at her reluctant host. "I can't."

A deep frown pinched his eyebrows together. "Can't? Or won't?"

She sighed, wondering how she could make him understand. Someone like him no doubt lived exactly as he wanted, answering to no one and living by his own rules. How could he possibly understand what her life had been like up to this point?

"A little of both, I think," she said, looking over at him. "If I go back now, I'll slip right back into the pattern of doing exactly what everyone always expects of me. For once in my life, even if it's only for a short while, I'd like to do things my way."

"And you expect to accomplish this how?"

"By getting a job, finding a place to live." She shrugged, wondering why she was even telling a total stranger her plans. It wasn't as if she was seeking his approval, for goodness' sake. Her days of seeking approval were over. "I haven't quite worked out the details."

He leaned forward and gave her a level stare. "You want some unsolicited advice?"

"Not really, but I expect you'll give it to me anyway," she muttered, reaching for the other slice of dry toast.

"Go home. As of right now, you have no car, no money, and—" his gaze slid over her, making her skin tingle as if he'd physically touched her "—no clothes."

"I realize it isn't exactly a stellar beginning," she said, rubbing her hands over her arms to ward off the unexpected chill chasing over her skin. "But I have to start somewhere. And if I could impose upon you for just a while longer, would you mind terribly—"

"You can't stay here," he said abruptly, and stood.

She shook her head. "I wasn't..." She'd planned on asking him if he'd mind finding a discount store open and picking up a few things for her so she'd at least have something besides his T-shirt to wear until she could get her bag. Until she had something decent to wear, she couldn't very well leave his apartment.

She frowned as an idea took root.

A very dangerous idea, but one she couldn't completely discard as inconceivable.

Why not? she wondered. If she was going to take control of her own life, why couldn't she ask him if she could bunk in his spare room for an extra night? Because the rules said she shouldn't? Because the rules said she couldn't possibly do something so rude as to impose on him?

Carly's Law: Don't be afraid to ask for what you need or want.

"I won't be any trouble," she blurted, before she lost her nerve. "I'll even share expenses until I can find my own place."

Cooper stared down at her, having serious doubts about her statement of being no trouble. Little Miss Cute and Curvy had been trouble with an underscored and capital "T" since she'd walked into his life. No. Not his life, his uncle's bar. The same bar he was close to losing if he didn't find a way to turn it around.

"It'll probably only be for a day. Two at the most," she said, sincerity banked in her innocent gaze.

The night she'd already spent under his roof was one night too many. He'd tossed and turned until dawn. Every time he closed his eyes, *she* drifted across his mind, an unwanted visitor in his home and his thoughts. The feel of her smooth as satin skin, the light floral scent of her hair, the way her long sooty lashes fanned against her cheeks while she slept had haunted his dreams. His very racy dreams.

"I like living alone," he lied, then walked back into the kitchen for more coffee. Truth be told, while he did enjoy his privacy, he'd never lived completely alone until recently, and reluctantly realized he missed having someone to talk to. Until he'd practically been forced by Hayden to join the service, he'd lived his life in this very apartment. After enlisting in the navy, he'd bunked with a bunch of other guys either in barracks, aboard a ship or in other places he'd rather not remember. There was Hercules, the cat his uncle had claimed kept a nonexistent rodent population under control, but Herc was a cat and didn't exactly qualify as a roommate, or a conversationalist.

"I promise not to get in your way."

He turned at the pleading note in Carly's voice. She stood next to the counter with her arms crossed, which caused the hem of his T-shirt to lift and reveal more of her smooth, lightly tanned legs.

He let out a rough breath. "I'm too busy. I have a bar to run." *I can't afford your kind of distraction.*

He felt himself wavering under the force of her full

and wide grin that had her eyes sparkling and the tempo of his heartbeat increasing.

"I won't be any trouble," she said. "Honest."

He didn't believe that for a minute. She was trouble of the worst kind, the kind that could easily drive him crazy...with need, if his physical reaction to her last night was any indication of his testosterone levels.

"I'll even help you with the bar."

He frowned. "I already have a waitress."

"I didn't see her last night."

"Karen's daughter is sick." The little girl suffered with asthma, and considering Karen had taken the child to the emergency room the previous night, the chances of her making her shift tonight were slim. Still, Sunday wasn't usually all that busy, except the Cubs were playing out of town and a few of his regulars would be in to watch the game on TV.

"What do you know about tending bar, anyway?" he asked, then quickly shook his head before he completely lost his sense, common or otherwise. "No. Forget it, Carly. Go home."

He walked out of the kitchen and headed into the living room to the entertainment center. He had two hours until he opened the bar, and he had things to do. Things that didn't include lusting after a tempting little distraction with a lethal body and a dangerous and determined glint in her ocean-blue gaze.

"I can't go home," she said from behind him. "At least not yet."

His hand stilled above the power button to the small stereo system. "You ever been a waitress?" he asked, looking over his shoulder for his common sense and finding only Carly and those soft-as-silk legs tempting him beyond reason.

"No." She crossed her arms again, drawing his attention to her breasts. "How hard can it be?"

He forced his mind out of the gutter. "The Wilde Side isn't some trendy, upscale club in a nice, safe part of town. The tips are lousy and the customers aren't looking for chitchat from some perky number like you. It's a neighborhood tavern that serves hard drinks to hardworking men. You won't fit in."

"How do you know that unless you're willing to give me a chance?"

He punched the button to the stereo and adjusted the volume low. "I just know."

"That's a cop-out."

A grin he wasn't really feeling tipped his lips. "It's my bar, Princess."

His uncle's bar, but his responsibility. Carly was a distraction, plain and simple. The fact that he couldn't get her out of his mind was more than enough reason for him to send her packing back to her safe world where people cared about her and were worrying where she'd gone.

With Karen off, he really could use the extra help, even if it was only to give him time to take care of other business matters regarding the bar. Matters that might allow the doors of The Wilde Side to remain open so he could keep his promise to Hayden, though it was a long shot.

"Why is this so important to you?" he asked before he could stop himself. Whatever happened to not caring?

She moved closer and trailed her finger along the entertainment center. "Before I go back home, I have to know I can make it on my own. I've never done anything important or even exciting my entire life. What everyone else wanted me to do, I did. I've always been the quintessential good girl. I've listened to and followed every single rule ever created. Boring and predictable. That's me," she said, then looked down at the dust-free pad of her finger with a frown before glancing up at him.

"All right," he reluctantly relented. "I could use the help for a couple of days. But if you're bored and looking for a vacation from staid and predictable, look elsewhere, Princess. The Wilde Side doesn't have what you're looking for."

"Oh, I don't know," she said, flashing him a grin full of sass that tightened his gut, instantly making him regret his decision. "I think spending some time on The Wilde Side could be very interesting."

Cooper didn't *even* want to go there. "It's only temporary," he managed, trying to shake a few wild images from his mind.

She stepped closer and looked up at him with those deep sea-colored eyes. Before he could guess her intent, Carly slipped her hand behind his neck and applied the slightest bit of pressure. "Thank you, Cooper," she said, her voice dropping to a husky whisper, sexier than anything he'd heard in a very long time. "You won't be sorry."

He was more than sorry when her sultry gaze shifted to his mouth. Against his will, his common sense fled faster than rats fleeing a sinking ship. There was no other explanation available, he thought, angling his head to capture her sweet lips beneath his.

4

Rule 4: Under no circumstances should a lady ever initiate advances.

CARLY PARTED HER lips. Her breath stilled, waiting, anticipating, willing Cooper to kiss her. In her heart, she knew his kiss would be one of the most sexually electrifying experiences of her boring and obedient life.

She couldn't explain what had come over her. The urge to kiss him was so strong, stronger than any sensual longing she'd ever felt. Just the thought of discovering the masculine secrets of that oh-so-sexy mouth made her skin tingle and her pulse pound in a heavy rhythm.

She leaned forward slightly, breathing in his rich male scent. Her lashes fluttered closed, but not before she saw the desire swirling in his eyes. Desire and heat and—

"We can't do this," he said abruptly, sliding his hand over hers and pulling it from around the back of his neck.

Desire, heat and...regret?

Disappointment slammed into her. She looked up into his eyes. Definitely regret.

What was wrong? He'd wanted to kiss her. She might have initiated the kiss, but he'd been a willing participant. Momentarily, at least.

"Why not?" she blurted. "We're both consenting adults."

He dropped her hand and took two steps back, widening the distance between them. "It's not a good idea."

Carly's Law: If it feels good, do it!

She planted her hands on her hips. "Why not?" she demanded again. He'd *wanted* to kiss her, too, so what was the problem? It wasn't as if she was some blushing virgin who'd never been kissed, although she had serious doubts about being kissed the way she imagined Cooper would kiss her. With intensity and demand. With a hunger he wouldn't be afraid to unleash, tempered by a gentleness so sweet she'd just melt.

And with more passion than she'd ever known existed.

He let out a rough breath and shoved his hands through his neatly trimmed hair. "Because."

She blew out her own frustrated stream of breath. "Oh, that's original." She crossed the living room to the sofa and plopped down on the cushion before she did something really stupid like throw herself at him. "You wanted to kiss me, Cooper. I know you did, so what's the problem?"

He straightened the already perfectly organized CDs, keeping his back to her. "We'd be borrowing trouble."

While she admired the view of his backside encased in soft denim, she wished he'd turn around so she could look into his eyes to see if he was telling her the truth or just being noble. "You wanted to kiss me," she told him again.

"That's beside the point."

She supposed that was about as much of an admission as she'd get out of him. "That's the *entire* point."

He finally turned to face her. Frustration replaced the desire she'd seen earlier. What she wanted to know was if it was the sexual kind.

He shook his head and walked to the recliner and sat. "It'd be a mistake." He settled his elbows on his knees, letting his hands dangle between his legs. "And I don't have time to get involved, Carly, no matter how tempting."

He managed to soothe her ruffled feminine pride. Except he was mistaken. She wasn't looking for anything long-term, or even involving.

A kiss.

All she'd wanted was a kiss.

But why now? And why Cooper, a virtual stranger, of all people?

She hadn't quite figured out the answer yet, but she knew she wanted one. A tongue-tangling one, filled with intense heat that would no doubt set her soul on fire and ignite a few other interesting places, as well.

While she might be intent on breaking a few rules and shucking convention for a while in her attempt to find some direction in her life and finally take control of her destiny, she had no intention of embarking on a full-blown affair with Cooper, no matter how stimulating she imagined it might be, or how satisfying. She wasn't completely without morals, and it had only been twenty-four hours since she'd left her groom at the altar.

But there was nothing wrong with a kiss, especially one with a man who'd made her skin feel all tight and hot the instant his eyes had darkened with desire.

She propped her bare feet on the coffee table, curling

her toes around the edge. "Who said anything about getting involved? A kiss, Cooper. One simple, harmless kiss."

Cooper doubted there'd be anything simple or harmless about it. The last thing he needed was to be lusting after some hot number looking to experience a little excitement, no matter how much sleep he'd lost during the night just thinking about her. That fact alone should have had him tossing Miss Brazen and Buxom out on her deliciously feminine posterior.

The Wildes had a history of obsessing over the opposite sex. As a kid, he'd watched his mother go from one man to the next. With each new love affair, Helena Wilde had been convinced that her new man was "the one." She would forget about everything else, her illegitimate son included.

His uncle hadn't been any better, and Cooper learned at an early age that love created distractions, often times with disastrous results. Those lessons had taught him well, so well that he tended to keep his distance, never allowing himself to get too close or too tied up by any one woman. That code had protected him for many years, and from what he'd seen thus far, despite her claims of non-involvement, Carly had involvement written all over her in pretty, feminine script.

"I already said you can stay here for a couple of days, but you're going to have to keep your hands to yourself, okay?" He ignored the voice in his head telling him he was a first-class idiot for not tasting her sweet, bow-shaped mouth when he'd had the chance.

She laughed, a deep, throaty sound that slid over his already heightened awareness, sharpening it to a fine point. "You know," she said, her voice infused with humor, "I never would have thought you were one of those look-but-don't-touch type of guys."

"You don't know me," he said with a deep frown. Oh, he wanted to touch her, all right, only he couldn't afford the very tempting distraction Carly represented, even for a brief period of time. He'd made a promise to his uncle to keep The Wilde Side going. The old-timers depended on the neighborhood tavern as a place to unwind after a hard day's work, and he refused to follow in the Wilde tradition of forgetting everything important just for a brief affair, no matter how enticing and promising. He wouldn't let the bar go without a fight, especially after sinking nearly every last dime of his savings into salvaging the place. And for what? he wondered caustically. A lost cause? The day of the local pub was over, at least for The Wilde Side. Thanks to his uncle's neglect, most of the locals were obviously taking their business elsewhere, more than likely to the more trendy nightspots the city had to offer.

Carly shrugged, drawing his attention back to their conversation and his gaze to her very full and unrestricted breasts. "You just strike me as the kind of guy who doesn't worry about following rules."

"I have rules." He stood in a vain attempt to keep his eyes *above* her neck. How could one woman make him want to forget his own code, a woman he didn't even know? The answer resided in his very defective genes. "And they don't include taking advantage of a woman," he said, using a harsher tone than he'd intended.

The sweet smile curving her sexy, very kissable mouth was filled with sass. "You would have hardly been taking advantage of me."

"You're in an emotional state," he said, attempting

to reason with her. He stuffed his hands into the back pockets of his jeans. "You would have regretted it later."

"I told you I wanted to experience life," she countered. Slowly, she swung her bare feet to the floor and stood. "I'm tired of following the rules, Cooper," she said, her voice dipping to a husky whisper as she advanced toward him with an I-want-you look turning her eyes a deeper shade of turquoise.

He swallowed. "Well, you can just forget about using me to break them."

She sighed, a big sound that caused her chest to rise and fall beneath her shirt. He nearly groaned.

She lifted her hand and lightly trailed her index finger over the edge of the pocket on his T-shirt. "That's too bad. Because I have a feeling it would have been a whole lot of fun."

Yeah, so did he. That was *his* problem.

He snagged her wrist and resisted the urge to smooth his thumb over the tender, silky flesh. Her eyes widened momentarily before a slow grin filled with feminine satisfaction curved her mouth. "Wanna have some fun, Cooper?"

Heat ignited in his belly and flew south. The woman could tempt a saint, and if there was one thing any Wilde was ineligible for, it was sainthood.

His grip on her wrist tightened slightly. God, he wanted to taste her. One kiss and he'd show her exactly the kind of fun she was asking for—the kind best played between the sheets. Too bad one kiss wouldn't be enough, at least for him. He'd seen for himself the kind of damage an affair could have on a Wilde.

"Forget it, Carly," he said roughly, before he followed through on every instinct screaming inside him to pull her into his arms and have that chickie-boom body pressed against him. He released his hold on her wrist before he tasted her lush mouth or smoothed his hands over her soft-as-silk skin. He turned and walked away from the sweetest brand of temptation he'd ever been offered, and settled instead for a cold shower.

CARLY SLIPPED A clean black T-shirt over her head and looked at her reflection in the narrow mirror behind the door of the small bedroom that would be her home for the next day or two. The hem of the shirt fell just above her knees, the sleeves falling below her elbows. She wrinkled her nose. The tent look wasn't quite what she was hoping to accomplish. She wanted sassy and sexy, not army surplus. No wonder Cooper had changed his mind about kissing her.

She let out a sigh. For someone trying to break brave new ground, she sure wasn't having much success in the masculine attention department. Of course, she really hadn't planned on venturing into an exploration of her sexuality, but darned if she couldn't get Cooper off her mind, especially the way he'd looked at her just before he'd put a stop to what she was positive would have been a serious sensual awakening.

She walked out of the bedroom and headed toward Cooper's room. He'd left, saying he'd needed to open the bar, before she had a chance to ask him if he'd mind doing a little shopping for her. She wasn't exactly snooping, since he'd left her no choice but to help herself to his wardrobe.

She stepped into his bedroom, and her gaze slid to the neatly made, king-size bed, where Hercules lay sprawled beneath a sunbeam. The cat lifted his head and glowered at her before yawning and closing his eyes to half slits.

She ignored the surly cat and headed toward the closet, but her attention strayed toward the bed again. The old Carly wouldn't steal into a man's bedroom and help herself to his clothes without permission. She would have kept the lustful thoughts that had tripped through her mind all to herself and wouldn't have impulsively and brazenly propositioned a man, especially one with more sex appeal than she knew how to handle. A man like Cooper would take and demand that she give without any hint of inhibition. She didn't necessarily think of herself as inhibited, but she was fairly certain she was a little out of her league when it came to flirting and teasing outrageously like a woman accustomed to making a few demands of her own.

Sweet Mary, what liberation. Always doing exactly what was expected of her was so…stifling. She giggled, thinking of herself as a butterfly still in the cocoon stage. Slowly, the stifling, constricting layers would peel away and she would emerge, new and reborn, stretching her wings and tasting freedom for the first time.

She put those silly thoughts aside and opened the door to survey the contents of Cooper's closet. Drumming her fingers on the doorjamb, she thought about how only two days ago she would have ignored the unexplainable need to taste Cooper's lips. And she most certainly would never have given in to the sensual awareness that had unexpectedly flared to life when he'd looked at her with all that intensity. The new Carly obviously had no such qualms about kissing a virtual stranger.

She let out a sigh. Just thinking of the deep, tongue-tangling kiss she missed out on had her knees going weak and her breasts feeling achy and heavy. Whether it was the thought of Cooper's kiss or the thrill of being so bold and naughty, she wasn't sure, but she was positive kissing him would be nothing short of sinfully delicious. Something she'd never felt with Dean. Not even when they'd made love.

Sweet Mary, what kind person was she? Twenty-four hours ago she'd been about to pledge her life to another, and now she was lusting after a man she barely knew. And enjoying it!

The thought of her abandoned bridegroom had her pushing her fingers through her still damp curls. Taking the coward's way out and running off the way she had was wrong, but she'd been backed into a corner and had panicked. Her flight-or-fight instincts had kicked in, and she'd failed by taking flight. But she *had* attempted to fight when she'd tried to tell Dean she didn't want to marry him. Even when she'd asked him if he was in love with her, he wouldn't give her a straight answer, nor would he admit that calling off the wedding was their only logical choice. Granted, he'd had a point in that a lot of people had gone to a great deal of trouble for their benefit. But wouldn't those same people rather see them happy and single instead of miserable and trapped in a marriage neither of them wanted?

She had serious doubts that Dean had been broken-hearted when he'd learned she'd disappeared without a trace. He'd probably been relieved. At least she hoped so.

She blew out a rough stream of breath, then jammed her hands on her hips. She had a decision to make. She could either wallow in guilt for the next few months as she attempted to pull her life together, or she could go forward and stop looking back to something she couldn't change.

No matter which way she looked at the situation, the truth remained that she and Dean hadn't been in love.

Carly's Law: Never marry for anything less than true love.

The time had come to put the past behind her. She'd made the right decision, no matter her method of approach. And until she could figure out the best way to deal with her family and explain everything to them so they would hopefully understand, she was staying in Chicago and was going to start over—on her own. Her parents had always told their daughters to be happy. When Jill had called off her wedding to Owen Kramer, they hadn't been upset, only concerned. In fact, they'd been downright relieved. The best she could hope for was the same kind of understanding and consideration. And with her parents, she'd no doubt have more than enough of both.

In the meantime, she had a few rules to break.

She pushed her guilt aside as best she could and began rifling through the contents of Cooper's closet. Everything was so...big. Of course, it had to be to cover that gloriously long, hard body of his.

She let out a little sigh and trailed her fingers along the hangers until she came to a white-and-green-striped dress shirt. She lifted the hanger off the rack and held the shirt against her. A very dangerous idea tugged at the new, naughty side of her emerging rule-breaking personality.

She gave in to the laughter bubbling up inside her as she continued her search for a belt and tie. She found what she needed, then headed back into the other bedroom to finish dressing. Lipstick and a tube of mascara were all she had in her little satin bag, so she pinched her cheeks to add a little color, scrunched her still damp curls until they were nearly dry, then stood back to admire her handiwork.

"Not bad," she murmured, fluffing her bangs using Cooper's comb. "Not bad at all."

She left the bedroom and headed downstairs to the bar. Cooper hadn't said anything about what time her shift was supposed to start, but she might as well get started...and not with just her new duties as a waitress.

By the time she was finished, Cooper would more than notice her. He'd be begging her for a kiss, and if she was lucky, a whole lot more.

As HE'D PREDICTED, the bar was relatively quiet. Marty and a couple of regulars quietly nursed cold beer while watching the Cubs lose to the Dodgers on the television screen set high on the wall behind the bar.

Cooper used the lull to organize a stack of invoices in order of importance. He didn't need a calculator to figure out that payables exceeded receivables once again. For the past six months he'd had to spend more than the bar was earning. What he needed was a plan, something that would draw customers into the bar and keep them coming back, but so far, he hadn't been able to come up with one.

Part of the problem, he knew, stemmed from aesthetics. Nothing about The Wilde Side had changed in the past forty years, but he couldn't see spending money for renovations when the customer base had dropped so dramatically in the past couple of years. But times were changing and the bar had to change with them or die a quiet death, the kind of death nobody but a few loyal folks would even care about or notice.

"How 'bout another cold one, Coop."

Cooper stuffed the unpaid invoices back into the file and shoved it beneath the counter before retrieving a fresh beer for Marty. He twisted off the cap and set the bottle in front of his old friend without comment.

"What's eating you, son?" Marty asked before tipping back the bottle.

Cooper braced his forearms on the bar and looked around. Nothing had changed since he was a kid. The same brown asphalt tiles he'd mopped for years still covered the floors. Dark brown wainscot and what had once been an off-white paint covered the plaster walls, separated by a four-inch plank of painted wood. A pair of pool tables newly recovered with green felt and a dozen round tables filled the space, while a variety of neon liquor signs graced the walls. The logos had changed, but the sentiment was still the same.

"Take a look at this place," he said, his tone conveying his thoughts. Sometime during the past thirty years, The Wilde Side had become a dump. No wonder Hayden's customers had gone elsewhere.

Marty shifted on the bar stool and glanced around the bar. "So?" he said when he turned back to face Cooper.

"There's no one here."

Marty's thick gray brows pinched together, deepening the crevices of his weathered face. "I'm here. Fred and Lou are here. We're somebody."

Cooper shook his head. "Three customers, Marty. Where the hell is everyone?"

Marty tipped back the bottle again then set it on the

damp napkin. "It's Sunday," he said with a shrug. "Things are always slow on Sundays."

"Not like this," Cooper argued quietly. "It never used to be that way. When I was a kid, I remember this place crammed full of people."

Marty folded his arms on the bar. "Things were different back then, Coop. When Helena was alive, she insisted that Sunday was family day. Folks used to be able to bring their kids and there were barbequed ribs and potato salad and baseball on the TV. Do that nowadays and you'll get arrested."

Cooper remembered those days. He remembered his mother spending every Sunday morning in the kitchen of their apartment upstairs making potato salad, gelatin salads and her own special, homemade barbeque sauce. The then single pool table would be used as a buffet, covered by a large plastic tablecloth. People from the neighborhood would bring side dishes and his uncle would give the kids free soda pop. During the holidays, there'd be two parties, one on the Saturday afternoon before Christmas, which catered to the kids of the neighborhood, complete with Marty dressing up as Santa and his mom as an elf handing out small gifts. That was followed by the annual Christmas party for the adults in the evening, with more than half the neighborhood in attendance. After Helena died, his uncle had tried to keep up the tradition, but it just wasn't the same without her, and he'd eventually stopped.

Cooper looked at his old friend and grinned. "You're right. If I tried something like that now, I'd be closed down."

"Times change, Coop," Marty said affectionately. "You gotta change with them."

He supposed the old man was right, but how? Maybe when Karen came back to work he'd take a few nights and check out the competition. He hadn't had much free time lately. Maybe a night or two with a change of scenery would give him back his perspective.

Marty let out a low whistle followed by a grin filled with male appreciation. "Well, will you look at that."

Cooper straightened and turned. His stomach bottomed out and his heart slammed into his rib cage. Carly flashed him a wickedly sexy grin combined with a sassy glint in her intriguing eyes, and even had the audacity to wink as she strolled toward him, slipping behind the bar as if she belonged there.

Her short bob of freshly washed platinum curls bounced and swayed as she moved. He couldn't help noticing she wore one of his old dress shirts, the top buttons undone to reveal just a hint of her smooth, full breasts. The old hunter green tie he'd forgotten he owned was knotted at the opening, drawing his attention to her chest. The high-heeled satin pumps he'd slipped off her feet last night enhanced the shape and length of those glorious legs, as did the tails of his shirt that cut high on her thigh, revealing a whole lot more skin he itched to smooth his hands over. She'd even liberated a wide leather belt from his closet, which she'd slung low on her hips. Hips that swayed enticingly with each step in his direction.

She stopped and looked up at him. "So? Where do you want me?"

Cooper could think of a lot of places, and not a single of one of them was behind the bar.

5

Rule 5: A lady will always allow a man to believe he knows what's best and must remember to keep her contrary opinions to herself.

CARLY RESISTED the urge to hand Cooper a napkin and tell him to wipe the drool from his chin. He wasn't really salivating, but all that male appreciation brimming in his eyes was just the reaction she'd hoped for when she'd gone digging through his closet for something to wear. She'd wanted him to notice her, and had he ever!

Until he frowned down at her. "What the hell do you think you're doing?"

She struggled to maintain her smile in the face of the ferocious frown making his angled features look harsh and unapproachable. As nonchalantly as she could, she said, "I was planning on working."

She didn't believe it possible, but his frown definitely deepened. "Watch the bar," he barked to an older gentleman, who lifted his half-empty beer in a saluted response.

Cooper manacled her wrist in his large, warm hand and pulled her along behind him. She could either follow or let him drag her wherever he planned to take her. The Neanderthal routine was definitely not flattering or warranted, but she opted to follow just the same.

The rapid click of her heels on the asphalt tiles mingled with the monotone voice of the sportscaster offering a play-by-play of the game on the television and the baritone chuckle of the man left in charge. Cooper stalked into a storage room and shut the door behind them with a snap before turning to face her.

"You gonna tell me what's up with the caveman act?" she asked, tugging her wrist from his grasp and backing up a step. She didn't fear him in the least, but he was so tall he towered over her. In order to look into that handsome, angry face, she had to tip her head so far back she was afraid she'd lose her balance.

"You're not wearing that getup in the bar, Carly. You'll get into trouble, and I don't need trouble."

She rolled her eyes and laughed. "There is absolutely nothing wrong with the way I'm dressed."

"You're half-naked," he said, shock and outrage evident in his deep, commanding voice.

"Oh, Cooper, get real." She waved her hand, dismissing his ludicrous statement. "I'm perfectly decent."

With the grumpy frown still in place, he braced his feet apart and crossed his arms over his wide chest. "The only thing you're wearing is a man's shirt. My shirt, too, I might add."

She wasn't going to apologize for snooping through his closet. Well, she hadn't really been snooping, just looking for something to wear besides her wedding dress or one of his T-shirts. "I've got dresses with less material than this," she countered, plucking at the shirt in question. "There's absolutely nothing indecent about my outfit."

"You're not wearing it," he stated. "Not in *my* bar."

She bristled. Not only was he being more than unreasonable, she didn't appreciate his high-handed atti-

tude. Her newfound independence didn't include suc-
cumbing to a man's demands, even if she had been
reduced to wearing his clothes. She propped a fist on
her hip. "And what do you propose I do wear?" she
asked with a sweep of her other hand down the length
of her outfit. "I don't have any clothes, remember?"

He blew out a stream of breath and uncrossed his
arms to plant those big hands on his lean hips. Her
gaze strayed to the denim covering his powerful-
looking legs. A pair of shorts would no doubt make
those long limbs of his look even more fabulous with
all that muscle rippling when he moved.

She forced her gaze back to his and added, "Besides,
the bar is practically empty. The guys watching the
game are at least my grandfather's age and look completely harmless to me."

He reached up and rubbed at the back of his neck as
if it was suddenly tense. No doubt he blamed her. "No
man is harmless when..."

His voice trailed off and he wouldn't look at her, but
stared down at the floor, instead. As if countering some
internal argument, he shook his head, then let out another harsh breath before his lips smoothed into a thin
line.

She narrowed the space between them and angled
her head to peer up at him. "When what, Cooper? No
man is harmless when...what?"

His gaze found hers and held it, his dark eyes filled
with an intense hunger that took her breath away.
"When a beautiful woman is prancing around half-
naked."

A slow grin curved her lips. Her tummy shouldn't
have fluttered just because Cooper said she was beautiful, but it did anyway. No man had ever called her

beautiful before. Cute, okay, she'd buy cute, but never beautiful. She was too round and curvy too be considered anything above cute.

"Thank you," she said quietly. At his questioning look she explained, "You paid me a compliment. Where I come from, it's customary to say thank-you."

He took a step back, the frown falling into place again. "You're changing the subject."

"What was the subject?"

"Your clothes. Or lack of them."

"This is just going to have to suffice until I can get my bag out of the car tomorrow." She let out a breath filled with resignation. "I'm not going to argue with you, Cooper. All the vital parts are well covered—"

"Barely," he interrupted.

"Oh big deal. So what if my legs are bare," she said in an exasperated tone and moved toward the door. All she had were white stockings, which would have been indecent with the lacy tops showing. She'd look like someone who frequented street corners and charged her dates by the hour. Independent did not equate to tasteless, and she did have standards. "Like I said, I have dresses with less material. Now, if you'll excuse me, I'm going back to the bar. I distinctly remember you offering me a temporary job in exchange for temporary room and board."

"No."

Carly stopped and turned, not liking the sharp tone of his voice. "No, I can't go back into the bar, or no, we didn't have an agreement?" she asked carefully. If Cooper knew her better, her even tone would have warned him he'd gone just a bit too far. He could argue with her all he wanted, but there was no way she was going to allow him, or anyone, to tell her what to do. Not any longer.

"No, you can't go back into the bar," he said, stepping in front of her. "Not dressed like that."

Carly's Law: Answer to no one except your own conscience.

Cooper nearly groaned when she shot him a look filled with determination and quiet anger.

"Watch me," she said, her voice a low warning.

He watched her, all right, in particular how the tails of his shirt swayed and fluttered against her rounded little bottom as she moved around him and walked toward the door.

He recovered quickly enough and shot ahead of her to block her escape.

Her turquoise eyes flashed with anger when she looked up at him. There was that spunk and fire he'd suspected was in her.

"What do you think you're doing?" she demanded.

Marty, Lou and Fred might be old enough to be grandfathers, but they were still men who appreciated a beautiful woman, especially one like Carly with more curves than an Indy racetrack and more fire than a Fourth of July exhibition. He was only trying to protect her, and it had nothing to do with the fact he didn't want anyone, in particular a bunch of old men, ogling her. "It's not safe for you to go out there."

"Don't be ridiculous," she chastised. "There are exactly three customers in the bar, and if by chance any one of them got the half-baked idea to chase the new waitress around the tables, I could easily outrun him. Now get out of my way, Cooper."

He ignored her warning demand and struggled against the strong urge to kiss her perfectly shaped mouth. "It'll get busier later and I can't baby-sit you all night."

"Baby-sit!" she exclaimed in outrage. She planted her hands on her hips, drawing his reluctant gaze to the top button of her shirt as if he was no better than a testosterone-laden youth. He was twenty-nine years old, for crying out loud. He'd had his share of women and shouldn't be behaving like the caveman she'd accused him of being.

"I don't need a baby-sitter, Cooper Wilde. In case you hadn't noticed, I'm a grown woman. And for the record, from what I can remember about last night, not a single one of your customers bothered me."

Oh, he'd noticed. Since she'd walked into the bar asking to use the phone, he'd noticed her, and worse, couldn't seem to get her out of his mind. Even when he'd thought she'd left and he'd never see her again, he'd thought about her. About her and that lethal body, both of which had haunted his dreams and his reality, and had him settling for a cold shower incapable of cooling his lust.

"That's because you had Benny and Joe playing bodyguard," he told her. "There aren't too many that'll take on those two. They're not here now and you're not trussed up in off-limits, virginal white. You're dressed like...like..."

Her eyes flared with brilliant color. "Like what, Cooper?" An unmistakable challenge laced her voice, just daring him to say the wrong thing.

"Like a grown woman," he said before he could stop himself. He narrowed the space between them and slid his hands over her slender waist and down to the slope of her hips. "Like a flesh-and-blood grown woman with curves in all the right places." A woman he couldn't get out of his mind. She was a distraction, one he couldn't afford, didn't need and sure as hell didn't want, but keeping his hands to himself was impossible.

One kiss, he told himself. One kiss and then the mystery would be solved and he could effectively evict her from his mind. One taste of her sweet, honeyed mouth and she'd be out on her lovely behind and remain strictly in the category of temporary roommate and part-time employee of The Wilde Side.

Her anger and exasperation faded, replaced by a sassy tilt to her lips. "You noticed."

"Oh yeah, Princess. I definitely noticed," he admitted. Noticed, admired and...obsessed. The defective Wilde gene left him with no hope of fighting his interest in Carly. Just like his uncle and mother, he was becoming completely entranced by the opposite sex.

"I was beginning to think you were blind."

He was beginning to think he was crazy. He didn't have time to play around with Carly, and she definitely wasn't the type of woman to embark upon a meaningless affair. She might be fiery and spunky, but Carly Cassidy had hometown girl written all over her hauntingly delectable body. While she craved to test her independence, the truth remained that she'd always done whatever her family expected of her, and breaking a twenty-four-year-old habit wasn't going to be easy. Eventually, she'd go back home, and he wasn't the guy to stop her. He wasn't the guy she needed in her life, especially when his own was such a mess. She'd be a temporary distraction, and no matter how fulfilling, one he refused to fall victim to, defective gene be damned.

His fingers pressed into her hips, but he couldn't set her away from him. Instead, he rocked her closer until their bodies touched. Her lashes swept downward as she lifted her lips to his, waiting, anticipating the first tentative brush of his mouth against hers.

One kiss, he sternly reminded himself as he gave in to the temptation and brought their lips together.

One taste to get her out of his mind.

One soft little moan from Carly and he was a goner.

She wreathed her arms around his neck, her full breasts brushing against his chest driving him wild. He'd only wanted a taste, but now that all that femininity was pressing against him, he had no choice but to deepen the kiss, even if he was torturing himself by collecting all of her hot and sweet flavors on his tongue. He caught another little feathery moan and just had to let his hands slide from her hips to her bottom to hold her even closer. A guy with a deficient gene pool lacked options, or self-control.

Had he honestly been foolish enough to think one kiss would really put an end to the mystery? He'd known her less than twenty-four hours and already he was following in the Wilde tradition. This all-consuming, fire-igniting kiss was only the beginning. A beginning that would end in heartbreak. He'd seen it happen too many times to ignore the truth. Too many nights he'd been the one to console his mother after some guy broke her heart and moved on to the next conquest. The constant craving he was already starting to feel for Carly was far too reminiscent, and he'd be damned if he'd end up like the Wildes before him.

He ended the kiss, instantly regretting the loss of heat generated between them. He struggled to ignore the heady impulse to pull her back into his arms and taste her again. Letting his hands fall to his sides, he stepped back until she had no choice but to release him.

"This can't happen," he said, then spun on his heel and left her alone in the storage room before he repeated history and fell victim to the sensual cast in her half-lidded gaze.

Too bad he had a bar to run, he thought, walking back into the common area. Another cold shower definitely held more appeal.

CARLY PRESSED her fingers to her lips. Sweet Mary, the man could kiss!

She let out a slow breath that did nothing to quiet her rapidly pounding heart or slow the blood still roaring in her ears. Her body hummed and she couldn't help wondering if Cooper made love the way he kissed. Demanding and tender, and so completely thorough.

This can't happen.

A short bark of abrupt laughter bubbled up inside her. "Wanna bet?" she murmured and grinned foolishly, propping her backside against a short stack of wooden crates. No way could Cooper claim disinterest after a kiss like that, she thought, tugging the hem of the shirt into place. He was plenty interested and more. Plain old-fashioned desire ranked pretty high on the list, in her opinion.

What she planned to do with that knowledge, she couldn't say, but just the thought warmed her clear to her toes and had her grin widening. She suspected Cooper would be an intense kind of lover. Just having all that intensity focused on her was enough to take her breath away, and she didn't think for a second she'd be disappointed, especially after the toe-curling kiss he'd just given her.

Stolen breath and curling toes would have to wait. She'd promised him a waitress in exchange for room and board for a couple of days, and sitting in the storeroom thinking about kisses and lovemaking was hardly keeping up her end of the bargain.

Feminine awareness heightened all over again when she walked back into the bar and found Cooper bent over a keg replacing tap hoses. She nearly sighed when he lifted the keg and slid it beneath the cabinet, the muscles and cords in his arms tightening and rippling from the weight.

He straightened and turned, giving her a resigned look. He might not be happy about her attire, but as she'd told him, there was absolutely nothing indecent about what she was wearing. "You never did tell me where you wanted me," she said.

Heat flared in his eyes telling her *exactly* where he wanted her, and it wasn't serving drinks to a handful of customers. The next forty-eight hours were certainly going to be interesting if every glance or word could easily be misconstrued as sexual innuendo.

"It's quiet," he finally said. "Why don't you just go upstairs and take it easy."

"Take it easy?"

He shrugged and turned away from her. "Read a book or watch a movie. Whatever. There's not much going on down here, anyway."

"You can't get rid of me that easily," she told him. Relaxing on a Sunday afternoon might be tempting since she did need to scan the papers for a real job and a place to live, but if she allowed him to chase her off now, he'd never let her back into the bar. Since the place was so quiet, unless Cooper suddenly had a change of heart and actually gave her real work to do, she'd have plenty of time to scour the want ads. "How about if I just clean up a little, and we'll see how that goes, okay?"

"I know how it's going to go," he groused. "Straight into trouble."

She ignored his surly attitude and went in search of a damp rag to wipe down the bar as she'd seen Cooper do the night before. Once she finished, she ventured from behind the bar and started on the dozen or so tables. They didn't need cleaning, but she wanted something to do besides stare at her quasi employer. Her imagination had enough ammunition without adding spark to a ready flint.

For the next hour, she busied herself under Cooper's watchful eye. Other than the few words he exchanged with the three men watching the Cubs game when they required additional refreshment, he was silent. He'd also been right about nothing much happening. The Wilde Side was anything but wild, and with the game in the last inning, the customers they did have would no doubt be leaving soon.

A short time later, with nothing left to clean, including the silent jukebox and neon signs scattered around the barroom, she wandered back behind the counter. Cooper sat on a stool watching her approach. She grinned and tossed the barely dusty rag into a tub of soapy water to soak.

Finding a spot between him and the corner, she propped her elbow on the old mahogany wood. "Is it always this dead?" The game had ended a good ten minutes ago and only one customer remained.

He let out a sigh and looked over his shoulder at her. "What's your point?"

She shrugged. "It's five in the afternoon on Sunday.

I always thought places like this would be hopping with men watching sports and getting rowdy while downing a few beers."

He shifted on the stool to face her, a self-satisfied and knowing grin on his lips. "Bored already, Princess?"

"I'm not bored," she said, drumming her fingers on the bar. "My mind is idle, so I've been doing a little math."

"Uh-oh."

She shot him a tolerant look. "You pay a waitress, but there's no one here for her to wait on. Factor in overhead like replenishing stock, utilities, maybe even repairs or rent, and I don't have to be an economist or an accountant to know The Wilde Side isn't pulling in a profit."

He turned his head slightly to the side. "You've been here less than two hours and you figured this out for yourself already?"

"It ain't rocket science, Cooper," she muttered with enough sarcasm to let him now she didn't appreciate his condescending tone.

He looked around the empty bar, then turned back to her. "No," he said quietly. "The bar isn't making a profit, but I've got no choice but to keep it open."

"Why?" she asked in an equally quiet voice before twenty-four-years of training took over and prevented her from prying. "I mean, I know it's none of my business, but if the bar is like this every day, isn't it going to go in the hole eventually?"

"It's already in the hole," the only remaining customer added, pushing a lock of thick salt-and-pepper hair off his weathered forehead.

Carly looked from the older gentleman to Cooper and the warning glare in Cooper's dark chocolate eyes.

"What are you doing to pull it out?" she asked, drawing Cooper's attention.

"Too damn much," the customer said before Cooper could answer. His tone was gruff, but there was no mistaking the affection banked in his weary blue eyes when he looked at Cooper.

Cooper let out a harsh breath and stood. "Marty, knock it off."

"You're not going to let it go under, are you?" she asked.

"He should," Marty complained. "Serve that useless SOB right if you did, son."

Cooper took two steps and stopped in front of Marty. "That's not going to happen, and you know it."

"He doesn't deserve what you're doing, Coop. And he sure as hell won't appreciate it, either."

Cooper shook his head and walked away.

"Who?" Carly called after Cooper, letting curiosity override good manners.

He glanced over his shoulder at her, and the warning in his eyes was unmistakable. "Stay out of it, Carly," he said in a sharp tone, then headed in the direction of the storage room.

She cast Marty a weak, apologetic grin. "I'm sorry," she said. "I didn't mean to upset everybody."

He gave a rough bark of laughter. "Everybody? You see anyone else sittin' here?"

Carly shook her head. No, and that fact did surprise her. The bar had been somewhat busy when she'd come in to use the phone last night, but now that she thought about it, it had been more of a steady kind of flow rather than a harried atmosphere she suspected most taverns experienced on a Saturday night.

"You want another beer, Marty?" she asked, sidling up to the bar opposite the older man.

He grinned and slid the empty bottle toward her. "Sure. Line 'em up, honey."

She reached into the cooler and found the brand he was drinking. "The name's Carly." She slipped a dry towel over the bottle, bit her lip and twisted hard on the cap.

"Thought it was Princess," he teased.

"No," she said with a grin. She thought about using a fresh napkin, but if the bar was losing money, a penny here and there might help Cooper. She set the beer on the damp napkin. "It's Carly. Carly Cassidy."

"Marty Davis," he said, extending his hand toward her. "Pleased to meet you, Carly Cassidy."

Carly busied herself wringing out the towel she'd used earlier, then worked on organizing the clutter beneath the bar. One thing she could say about The Wilde Side was that it was clean. Of course with the lull in customers, cleaning was about the only thing a bartender or waitress had to do to fill their time.

"It's not his bar," Marty said suddenly.

Carly looked up from her task. "I don't understand." She thought Cooper *owned* The Wilde Side, especially since he kept referring to it as *his* bar.

"The Wilde Side belongs to Coop's uncle," he explained after a glance toward the storage room. "Hayden's...out of town and no one knows where to reach him."

She folded the damp towel in the same pattern she'd seen Cooper do earlier. "That's not very responsible." Oh, she was a fine one to pass judgment about responsibility.

Marty lifted the bottle to his lips and paused. "No

one ever said Hayden Wilde was responsible," he said. "Coop came back to look out for Hayden and Hayden took off. It's not the first time."

Questions filled her mind, like where was home for Cooper if he came *back* to Chicago? And if he wasn't the bar owner, what did he do for a living?

"I think what Cooper's doing is very commendable," she told Marty.

The old man grunted. "Damned stupid if you ask me. 'Specially when the boy's heart is elsewhere."

She absently drummed her fingers on the stainless steel counter beneath the mahogany bar. Cooper's heart was elsewhere?

"You gonna stick around a while, Carly?" Marty asked, settling his bottle back on the napkin.

"Just for a day or two," she answered absently, her mind on the dozens of questions she had about her temporary employer and landlord. Who was the man who'd kissed her so passionately?

She was attracted to Cooper. She couldn't deny that little fact. Desire and tension had swirled between them, and she'd be a liar to suggest anything less existed. But how could she even consider getting physical with a man she didn't know? She'd *thought* she'd known him, sort of, or rather was getting to know him...until her conversation with Marty.

This can't happen.

Sweet Mary, no wonder he'd ended their kiss so soon.

His heart was elsewhere? Was Cooper Wilde, the man she'd been lusting over since she'd walked into the bar last night, *married*?

6

Rule 6: A lady may allow a man to kiss her hand at the end of their first date.

COOPER'S ATTEMPT to work off some steam with physical labor was failing. For the past six months he'd tried to keep the bar open, because in his opinion, he owed it to his uncle. The Wilde Side would belong to him one day, and it'd be nice if there was something of it left by the time he actually inherited the bar from Hayden. At the rate things were going, the only thing he'd receive as his legacy was a stack of unpaid bills.

He hefted cartons of Beefeater gin and Smirnoff vodka into his arms and carried them across the storage room closer to the door, then went back for the cases of Kessler's and Seagram's whiskey. Inventory was running low. Replenishing the stock was as simple as an order to the suppliers, but paying those invoices at the end of the month was an altogether different matter. Unless he found a way for the bar to earn some money, he'd have no choice but to pour more of his own savings into the business, and he could forget about recouping the cash he'd already expended.

The door opened and he didn't need to turn around or even look over his shoulder to know Carly had walked into the storage room. His feminine detection equipment was in top working order and zeroed in on her allure like a heat-seeking missile.

"Who's watching the bar?" he asked, his voice a bit harder than he'd intended. Frustration, particularly of the sexual kind, did that to a guy.

"Marty," she said, closing the door behind her. "Not that there's anyone out there for him to watch."

He took a deep breath and let it out slowly. "Thank you for the observation, Dr. Watson," he muttered, lifting the cases of whiskey and adding them to the others he'd already moved.

She leaned against the door, her hands pressed against the smooth wood and tucked behind her bottom. A kaleidoscope of emotions crowded her gaze, ranging from anger to disappointment.

"Did you want something?" he asked her, irked that she was looking at him as if he ranked right below pond scum.

Her eyes flared with brilliant color, warning him she was ticked about something.

"Are you married?" she asked. From her statement and the accusation in her voice, it didn't take much to figure out what had her riled this time.

"Am I what?"

She pushed off the door and advanced toward him, stopping a few inches away. "Married," she said in that same accusatory tone he was beginning to dislike.

She folded her arms and cocked her hip slightly to the side, causing the hem of his shirt to hike up even higher on her smooth thighs. "Married," she said again. "As in that's why you *can't* kiss me."

He laughed, because the idea of marriage was ridiculous. He'd spent the past eleven years moving from one place to the next, taking whatever undercover assignment was given to him. There'd been no one, other than Marty and maybe his uncle, who gave a rat's behind where he'd been or even cared about the horrendous things he'd seen as a navy SEAL. Congress could call it what they wanted, war was war even if they did stick a pretty, politically correct, police-action label on it.

"Where'd you get an idea like that?"

She narrowed her spectacular eyes. "I'm not stupid, Cooper. The usual reasons a man *can't* kiss a woman are that he's either gay or married. You're obviously not gay, so married makes the most sense."

He shook his head, thoroughly confused—only one of the states of mind he was quickly coming to realize was more common than not when it came to dealing with Carly. The other was much more interesting. "What the hell are you talking about?"

"'This can't happen,'" she mocked in bad baritone imitation. "It's obvious. Marty said your heart was elsewhere. You've got to be married, or engaged or in a relationship."

He chuckled again and turned away to finish moving the inventory. "So that's what's got you in such a snit."

Marriage wasn't for him, and he knew it. His mother had never married, nor had Hayden, although both of them enjoyed cavorting with the opposite sex to the point that the rest of their lives took a back seat, even the important things, like their livelihood or Helena's own son. He'd accepted his illegitimate status a long time ago, but had handed out his share of black eyes to the kids who dared call him a bastard. Marriage was just never important to the Wildes. At least not as important as a good time.

"I'm not in a snit," she said in a haughty tone. "I just don't think you're a very nice person going around kissing women and turning them all inside out with...with...well, never mind. You shouldn't be doing that when you're already married. Adultery is one of the Top Ten, you know."

Curious, he turned around to find a becoming blush staining her cheeks. Turned her inside out, huh? He liked the sound of that, especially since she had him tied up in so many knots he didn't think he'd ever get himself untangled.

He narrowed the distance between them. God, she looked adorable when she was irritated with him. Her eyes flashed with color and the mouth he couldn't stop thinking about kissing again was pursed into the most lovely little pout he'd ever seen. "I'm not married, Princess," he said quietly. "I never have been and probably never will be."

Hope replaced the irritation in her gaze, and he nearly groaned. Hope he didn't want. Hope he didn't need. It led to unaffordable distractions he refused to allow to be his downfall, regardless of his ancestry.

"You're not?"

He turned away from the hopeful note in her voice and moved to the far end of the storeroom before answering her. "No."

"Why?"

"Why what?"

"Why won't you ever get married?"

He shot an irritated glance over his shoulder. "Anyone ever tell you, you ask a lot of questions?"

She had the nerve to smile. "All the time," she said, hoisting herself on top of a short stack of wooden crates. "Now answer mine. Why do you think you'll never get married?"

"You wanted to work, so why don't you go back to the bar and keep an eye on things."

She crossed her legs and braced her hands behind her. His gaze followed the smooth line of her legs, and he felt the first stirring of desire. He was cursed. Doomed to follow in the same footsteps as the rest of the Wildes.

"You didn't answer my question."

He pulled another carton from the back of the storeroom and moved it with the others. "I never stay in one place long enough."

"Where are you from?"

"Chicago," he answered, struggling to keep his mind on the physical labor of moving stock and not the other more interesting physical acts that refused to leave his thoughts. He couldn't help himself. Not only did he have a defective gene, but how could he think of anything else when her legs were just too darned smooth and silky? He knew. Lord, how he knew. Removing those fantasy-arousing stockings from those shapely limbs the night before had been pure torture.

A longing ache gripped him. Just one touch, he thought as he walked past her to the rear of the storeroom again for another carton.

"Marty said you came *back* to look out for your uncle. That pretty much indicates you live elsewhere."

She dangled her foot, slightly swinging her leg and drawing his attention like a magnet to metal. "That old man talks too much," he complained. What harm would there be in easing off that shoe and smoothing his hands over her slender feet, up her shapely calf, along her knee and higher over her thigh to her hip?

Surely it wouldn't be the end of the world if he continued his exploration to palm her breast in his hand and feel her nipple bead against his fingers.

"Be that as it may," she said, "where *do* you live?"

"Above the bar," he answered shortly. *Work*, he thought. *Just keep working and don't think about her.*

He hefted three cartons this time.

"What about before that?"

He set the cartons near Carly's dangling foot and let out a harsh breath. She wasn't wearing store-bought perfume, but he caught a delicate scent that could only be described as feminine, and just as alluring, pushing him to the edge of temptation. "If you must know, I was in the navy."

She started twisting her foot in little circles. He watched in fascination as the muscles in her calves worked, gliding beneath the surface of her skin with each movement.

"Oh." Something in her voice changed, but he couldn't quite put a name to it. "Was? You're not any longer?"

With every ounce of willpower he possessed, he dragged his gaze from her legs to her face. That was his first mistake. Interest lined her gaze, the sexual kind he was powerless to ignore. When it came to Carly, all he thought about was sex.

He committed his second mistake the minute he gave in to temptation and touched her. "I was discharged about six months ago." He kept his gaze locked with hers and settled his hands on her legs. Gently, he eased her knees apart and stepped between them so her legs bracketed his hips. "Why do you care?" he asked, when she made no move to push him away.

"I'm just...curious," she said, her voice barely above a whisper. Now why did he know she was no longer talking about his past, but something much more interesting and fulfilling?

He shifted his hands to her bottom and carefully scooted her forward. "Curiosity killed the cat," he murmured. If he was a feline, he'd be dead by now.

He breathed in her intoxicating scent anyway.

"So where's your uncle?"

Unable to stop himself, he dipped his head and nuzzled her neck. She trembled, sending his overactive libido skyrocketing. "Now there's a question I can't answer for you, Princess," he murmured against the warmth of her skin.

She pulled back to look at him, surprise evident in her lovely expression. "You mean he just took off and didn't tell you where he was going?" she asked, her voice filled with an indignity that touched him in a way he hadn't expected. Deep inside, in a place unused for too many years.

"Something like that," he said, running his hand along her spine. "I don't want to talk about my uncle. Tell me about this twisting inside out thing, instead."

She blushed again. "Oh. That."

"Yeah, that."

She shrugged. "It was...nothing."

He shook his head. "Uh-uh, Princess. I answered your questions. Now answer mine."

She let out a slow breath and gave him a sly glance. "What do you want to know?"

Ducking his head, he zeroed in on the spot behind her ear that had her trembling in his arms again. "About this twisting thing," he said, nipping at her earlobe, then soothing the spot with his tongue.

Carly sucked in a sharp breath and attempted to recite the Beatitudes.

Blessed are...

Blessed are...

Blessed are Cooper and his wicked tongue.

"How about if I tell you about my family, instead?" she asked in a vain attempt to get her mind off the heat pooling in her belly.

"Not interested," he whispered, his hot breath fanning her ear and making her shiver.

"My father's a minister," she said anyway.

"Hmm...." He nipped at her earlobe, not the least bit distracted, then trailed a fiery path over her throat and upward to nip at her chin. His hands moved from her back to her rib cage, his thumbs brushing the underside of her breasts, making her nipples tighten beneath the restraining cups of her corset.

He brushed his mouth lightly over hers. "So you know all about sin then, don't you, Princess?" he murmured against her lips.

If this was sin, then she'd gladly take the journey into the inferno. She didn't need a guide to show her where she'd end up, either. Right smack in the middle with all the other lustful sinners.

"Yes," she answered in a breathless whisper. The heat in her tummy spread through her limbs, making her feel tight and hot and needy.

"Is it true you can sin with your mind and not your body?"

"I've never believed in mind and body separatism."

"But can you?" The heat and passion in his voice fueled her own. His hands moved upward to cup her breasts and she arched toward the warmth of his touch.

"Oh, yes," she whispered, unsure whether she was answering his question or urging him onward.

He pulled back to look down at her. All the fire, all the passion coursing through him flared in his dark eyes, adding gold flecks that reminded her of hot, molten lava. "Then I'm in dire need of salvation," he rasped, before ducking his head to capture her lips in her second breath-stealing kiss of the day.

His tongue swept between her lips in long sensuous strokes, raising her desire to a feverish level. Something she couldn't begin to understand was happening between them. They were virtual strangers, but she responded to Cooper as if she'd known him intimately forever. He set her soul on fire and made her feel things that until now she'd only heard about from her sisters. Cooper's kisses exceeded pleasant and shot straight to hot and demanding.

She answered the demands of his mouth with a few of her own, looping her arms around his neck and bringing their bodies closer together. He instinctively knew what she needed and inched her bottom closer until nearly every inch of their bodies were touching. His marble-hard chest felt glorious against her sensitized breasts. His scent, his heat surrounded her, holding her captive in a prison from which she had no desire to escape.

His hands eased down her legs and back up again, the rhythmic motion adding fuel to an already burning fire. When his hand skimmed beneath the hem of her shirt, his fingers brushing against the elastic band of her panties, she quivered with urgent sensations unlike anything she'd ever known.

"Marty said I'd find you in—"

Startled beyond her wits, Carly jerked back. The

band on her panties snapped loudly against her skin as Cooper abruptly did the same, leaving the woman who'd just barged in on them with little doubt exactly what they were doing in the storeroom.

"Excuse me," she said, her voice infused with humor. "I didn't realize you were busy, Coop."

"We're not," Carly said, attempting to straighten her shirt as nonchalantly as possible. Considering the tails were bunched around her thighs, inconspicuous she wasn't.

Cooper took a step back and ran a hand through his closely cropped hair. "We were just...uh, taking inventory," he said lamely.

Taking inventory? Of what? Each other's bodies?

"This is Carly," he said to the tall, slim woman dressed casually in leggings and a thigh-skimming polo shirt. "She'll be helping out for a couple of days. Carly, this is Karen."

Carly offered a weak grin to Karen, who looked at her with interest brimming in her rich brown, almond-shaped eyes.

"How's your daughter?" Carly asked, not quite knowing what to say. She'd never been caught in a situation like this and didn't have a clue how to handle it other than to pretend that she and Cooper weren't doing anything illicit. A preacher's daughter didn't go around sinning every day—at least Richard Cassidy's daughters didn't. She couldn't say the same for Emily Burton, the Nazarene minister's daughter. The boys in school hadn't called her Easy Emily for nothing.

Karen smiled warmly. "Thanks for asking. She's much better." To Cooper she said, "I was hoping you wouldn't need me for a few days. They want to keep Elizabeth in the hospital and run some tests. We finally got a decent doctor who thinks her asthma could be a result of allergies.''

"Sure," Cooper said. "Take as long as you need."

Relief entered Karen's eyes. "Thanks, Coop. It'll just be a couple of extra days. I promise."

"No problem."

"Thanks," Karen said again, then swung the door open. "Nice to meet you, Carly."

Still embarrassed, Carly grinned sheepishly.

Karen turned to go, then stopped and turned to face Cooper. "I almost forgot. Marty said you'd better get your backside out there unless you want to put him on the payroll." She laughed and closed the door, leaving Carly alone with Cooper.

Carly slid off the crates. "I'll go," she told him, and headed toward the door hoping Cooper wouldn't think to stop her. She needed some time alone, or rather, time away from Cooper, because the man was definitely bad for her. She reached for the door and frowned. Bad for the old Carly. Not the new and improved one who lived by her own laws, grabbed on to life with both hands and enjoyed every moment given to her.

Carly's Law: There's nothing wrong with making love to a man who turns you inside out.

"We're not finished, Carly," Cooper said. There was no threat in his voice, just enough wicked promise to jump start her pulse all over again.

With her hand on the doorknob, she looked over her shoulder at him. "We're not?" she asked, thrilled to see that the promise in his voice matched the one in his gaze.

His mouth tipped up into a grin. "We've got a sinful discussion to finish."

The still-simmering heat in her belly ignited, leaving her knees weak and her insides quivering with forbidden anticipation. Heaven help her, she'd wanted his attention, and now that she had it, she just wasn't sure what to do. Be careful what you wish for, she thought.

She couldn't form an answer to save her life, so she turned and pulled the door open, anxious to put some distance between herself and the sinfully sexy man who turned her inside out with as little as a tilt to his wickedly delicious mouth.

"Princess?" he called, his voice filled with more sensual demand than she had the power to ignore. No one had *that* much willpower. "Answer one question for me."

She waited, mesmerized as he slowly walked toward her. His rascal of a grin deepened and her pulse quickened. She stared up at him as he lifted his hand and gently smoothed his knuckles down her cheek in an infinitely tender gesture that snagged her heart.

His grin faded and his eyes filled with such seriousness her breath lodged in her throat. "Are you a virgin, Carly?"

She was stunned. No teasing light entered his gaze, and nothing tugged that heavenly mouth back into a grin. He was dead serious.

"No, Cooper," she told him honestly, surprised his question didn't make her blush as if she was pure and untouched. "I'm not." She didn't have gads of experience, either, but she had made love to her former fiancé.

"Good," he said, dropping his hand to his side and grinning like the devil. "Because we couldn't make love if you were."

He brushed past her, and Carly gripped the doorjamb with both hands for support as she watched him saunter down the short hallway to the common area of the bar as if he hadn't just tipped her world upside down.

gerously, I sent hands down my spine as she walked past him, settling down the story behind my head now? a the cellular price of cre line bar as if he hadn't said. I could not avoid seeing down.

_____ *7* _____

Rule 7: Don't forget about Rule 3.

THANKS TO Cooper making the trip to the car dealership first thing in the morning for her bag, Carly
slipped into her own pair of faded blue jeans and
sighed contentedly. Finally rid of the confines of the
corset she'd had no choice but to wear until she had her
own lingerie, she gratefully secured the front hook on
her satin bra and then tugged her favorite, faded Hard
Rock Café T-shirt over her head. Wearing her own
clothes felt heavenly and would give her tons more
confidence when she faced Cooper.

After his mind-blowing statement yesterday afternoon, she needed all the confidence she could muster.
Stunned could only describe how his parting remark
had left her. Stunned and even more incredibly aware
of the man who so easily set her soul on fire. Not exactly the reaction of a woman determined to set her
own rules and live life by the moment.

Following his far too intriguing remark, he'd kept
his distance and even had the audacity to pretend he
hadn't carelessly tossed her universe into another
sphere. As she'd waited on the few customers who'd
come into the bar early Sunday evening, she could feel
him watching her. Struggling to ignore his dark, intense gaze at the bar, and later in the apartment, had

proved more difficult than she imagined. All she could think about was Cooper and his threat that they *would* make love.

A threat she couldn't ignore if her new, independent life depended on it.

After blowing her hair dry and applying a scant amount of makeup, she finally left the small, spartan bedroom and headed into the living room in search of a newspaper. She'd told Cooper she'd only stay with him one or two days, which meant she needed to find suitable employment and an apartment if she planned to stay in Chicago.

When she'd left Homer so abruptly, she really hadn't had a destination in mind, but had merely wanted to get as far away from everything familiar as humanly possible. She'd felt trapped and stifled. Because Dean refused to listen to her or even consider that they were being pushed into a marriage neither of them wanted, she'd had no choice but to take drastic steps to maintain her freedom.

Or maintain her identity?

She didn't know any longer, but she did know that calling off the wedding had only solved one of her problems. In less than three months she was due to start teaching music at Homer High. She'd graduated from Indiana State with a degree in modern dance, and as her father had explained when she expressed her uncertainty about the job, it made sense that she teach music. She'd done as expected and accepted the position because her sister Wendy had arranged it for her since Mrs. Oliver was retiring. Teaching music in a small-town high school was the last thing Carly wanted to do with the rest of her life. Nor did she want to end up like Mrs. Oliver, whose idea of fun was directing the ninth grade boys' choir or tending to her prize-winning tulips every spring. She wanted more from life than worrying about puberty ruining those young sopranolike voices before the annual Christmas festival. Maybe she even wanted to be more like her older sister, Jill. Jilly didn't conform to the demands of family, but had moved nearly two thousand miles away to Los Angeles, where she worked as a criminal attorney.

The living room was deserted except for Hercules lounging lazily on the seat of the recliner. She let out a relieved sigh and ventured into the kitchen for coffee, then carried it back into the living room with the newspaper she'd found folded neatly on the small dining room table. After dropping off her bag, Cooper had said he had some errands to run before opening the bar that afternoon, and thankfully, she'd have some time alone, to think.

And *not* about Cooper.

Yeah, sure.

Attempting to ignore her conscience, she settled on the sofa with her coffee and spread the newspaper on the table. Hercules glared at her for disrupting him from his slumber. All she'd seen him do was sleep, or follow Cooper whenever he walked into the kitchen. "Don't worry, Hercules," she told the cat over the rim of her cup. "I'll be out of here by tomorrow."

Thirty minutes later she looked over at the sleeping cat and muttered, "Maybe not."

She heard a key slip into the lock followed by Cooper walking into the living room with plastic shopping bags in his hands. When her heart stuttered behind her ribs, she wasn't the least bit surprised. The man affected her, and she'd just better get used to it, because fighting her attraction to him was as futile as a child trying to catch Santa swooping down the chimney on Christmas Eve.

He shifted the bags in his hands. Her gaze strayed to his corded forearms and she would've sighed with pleasure if she wasn't so disgusted and disappointed with the enormous cost of rent in Chicago combined with slim employment opportunities.

"What are you wrinkling your nose about?" he asked, heading into the kitchen.

She left the newspaper open on the coffee table and followed him. "The cost of living. Have you seen what apartments are going for in this city?"

He chuckled and set the bags on the counter. "It's Chicago," he said. "What did you expect?"

She poured herself a second cup of coffee then propped her backside against the counter to watch Cooper pull grocery items from the bags. She hid a smile behind her mug when she spied a variety of flavored teas, touched beyond measure by his thoughtfulness. "Certainly not four figures for a basic one-bedroom apartment. And that's not even overlooking the river."

He opened a narrow pantry cabinet and stacked the teas inside. "Being an independent woman has its price."

"Very funny," she said, peering around his shoulder. The teas were in alphabetical order.

"So what are you going to do?" he asked, arranging the prepacked meat he'd purchased in an orderly pile. "Go home?"

She set her cup on the counter. "Let me help," she said, picking up the packages of beef and chicken, carrying them to the freezer. "I can't go home. Not yet."

"There are people who care about you, Carly," he said, opening the freezer for her. "Do you realize how lucky you are?"

The longing in his voice snagged her attention. Who was Cooper Wilde? She knew he'd been in the navy, and that he'd come home to help his uncle, but other than the fact that he made her long for things she'd never before experienced, she knew next to nothing about who *he* was as a person. His wants, his needs, his goals and dreams. They were all a mystery she wouldn't mind unraveling.

She set the meat in the freezer and moved back to the counter for the package of thick pork chops. "Oh, I know I'm lucky, but I can't go home. All my life I've always..." She watched in amazement as he rearranged the packages she'd just put into the freezer, carefully placing them in order of type—she peered closer—and cut. "I've already told you this. Sweet Mary, Cooper. You are anal."

He tossed her a tolerant look and took the pork from her. "I like things orderly. You didn't tell me why you ran away from your own wedding. What happened?"

She shrugged. "We weren't in love."

"You should've called it off sooner instead of waiting until you were ready to walk down the aisle."

She watched him arrange the pork in the freezer in the same way he'd done the beef and chicken, and shook her head. "I tried to tell Dean, but he wouldn't listen to me. We grew up together and started dating in high school. I went off to college and when we continued to see each other, everyone just sort of assumed we'd get married. I guess Dean and I did, too, because when he proposed it all seemed so logical at the time that I didn't even consider turning him down."

He closed the freezer and returned to the groceries still scattered on the counter. "But?" he asked, not looking at her.

"But we weren't in love with each other." She braced her hands behind her on the counter and lifted herself onto the Formica top. "We loved and cared about each other, but not in a way that meant we should get married. There just wasn't that...I dunno—" she shrugged "—spark, I guess."

"There's more to marriage than sparks," he said, adding the canned vegetables to the pantry cupboard. She didn't need to look to know they too would be in alphabetical order.

She laughed and slipped a wayward curl behind her ear. "How would you know? You're not even married, and yesterday you told me you had no intention of ever getting married."

He closed the cabinet and looked at her. That longing she'd heard in his voice showed in his eyes, heightening her curiosity. "I never said I had no intention of getting married, just that I probably never would."

"Don't you believe in happily ever after, or finding that one special person to share your life with?"

He looked away. "Not really."

"Did someone hurt you?"

"No."

"What happened?" she asked, her curiosity overriding her good manners once again. She figured if she wanted to learn more about him, she'd better start taking the direct approach and ask questions that would require him to provide more than a monosyllable for an answer.

He folded his arms and propped his shoulder against the pantry cabinet. "I wasn't the one who was hurt," he said. "I just saw what happened to my mother. She was searching for a prince but ended up with jerks who used her and then moved on, leaving her behind with a broken heart. My uncle isn't any better. When it comes to the opposite sex, the Wildes have a lousy track record."

The glimpse he'd given her took her by surprise, making her realize exactly how sheltered her life had really been. Living in the same small town all her life, surrounded by people who loved her and cared about her, she'd never been subject to the kind of disappointment and heartache Cooper was referring to. Even if he hadn't experienced that disappointment or heartbreak himself, it made sense that he'd be hesitant to give his heart to a woman. Examples were strong motivation.

She folded the plastic bags and looked over at him. "So you think this applies to you as well, is that it?"

"You can't change history, or genetics," he said, pushing off the cabinet. He strolled past her and out of the kitchen, signaling an end to the brief glimpse into the real Cooper.

She didn't find him in the small dining room or the living room, so she ventured deeper into the apartment. A movement caught her attention. She investigated, finding him unloading the contents of his pockets into a square box atop a tall chest of drawers.

She leaned against the doorjamb and crossed her feet at the ankles. "You never did tell me what happened to your uncle."

"He took off. With a woman."

"Really?" she said, pushing away from the door. She entered his bedroom and sat on the edge of the king-size bed. "And he left you to take care of his bar?"

"Something like that." He turned and stopped, staring at her. The look in his eyes when he found her sitting on his bed could only be described as...fear? Fear of what, she wanted to know. Her? After what he'd said yesterday about making love, the idea of him being afraid of her was laughable.

"Look, I really don't want to get into this, Carly."

She wasn't about to let him escape her interrogation. Getting answers out of Cooper wasn't the easiest thing she'd ever attempted, but she wanted, no needed, to know more about this man who tipped her world upside down and made her look forward to breaking every single rule she'd ever lived by.

"Marty said it wasn't the first time your uncle has done something like this," she said. "He even implied your uncle lied to you to get you home."

He sighed and dropped onto the bed beside her. "You're not going to let this go, are you?"

She flashed him a wide grin. "I'm curious."

He made a noise that resembled a grunt of disapproval.

"Well?" she prompted.

He leaned forward, bracing his elbows on his denim-clad legs, clasping his dangling hands between his knees. "It's my own damn fault," he said after a moment of examining the worn Oriental rug. "I should have known better, but Hayden said he needed me. About a year ago he had a heart attack. Nothing too serious, but enough to scare us both. I thought he was sick when he called again six months ago. He'd told me he needed me to come home for an extended period, so instead of visiting the retention officer and reenlisting for another six years, I went for a discharge. I came home, then Hayden took off with some woman again, convinced he was in love with her. I haven't heard from him since."

She slipped her hand over his forearm and gave him a gentle squeeze she hoped he took for comfort. "Again?" she asked. "He's done this kind of thing before?"

He glanced down at her hand then up at her and nodded. "I was only fifteen the first time."

"How long was he gone?"

"About a month," he said.

"Oh my God," she whispered, appalled that anyone could desert a child for any length of time. Granted, a fifteen-year-old boy hardly qualified as a child, but Cooper certainly hadn't been of an age where he should've been left alone to fend for himself.

"I survived," he said with a careless shrug.

She didn't buy his no-big-deal routine for a nanosecond. Not when she'd caught a glimpse in his gaze of old wounds still tender. Her heart went out to the young man he'd been, deserted by the only person he'd had in the world to see to his well-being.

"I think what you're doing is very noble, Cooper. Especially after what he did to you. You gave up your career to take care of your uncle's business, and that's very commendable."

"There's nothing noble or commendable about it." He stood and crossed the room to the open window. "I wanted an excuse to leave the service, and Hayden gave it to me, even if it was under false pretenses."

He kept his back to her, giving her a perfect view of his even more perfect backside.

"What are you going to do?" she asked him.

His abrupt bark of laughter fell dramatically short of humorous. "What I've been doing," he said, a trace of bitterness in his velvety voice. "I promised Hayden I'd keep the bar open until he gets tired of chasing skirt and comes home. I've tried not too think too much about what's going to happen after that."

Cooper was too organized for her to believe he was simply biding his time, living a rootless day-to-day existence dependent upon the whims of another. Any man who spent time alphabetizing the meat in his freezer had to have a plan or two for his future.

"I doubt that," she said, now that she'd seen past the barriers he used to surround himself. "You have to have a plan, Cooper. Your personality demands it. Are you going to take over the bar permanently?"

"I've lived most of my life in this apartment and in that bar," he said, a frown pulling his sable brows together over the bittersweet expression banked in his gaze. "The Wilde Side is where I started, and it sure as hell isn't where I plan to end up. I was planning to start my own security company once I retired from the navy, but now that'll have to wait."

"Because of Hayden's disappearance?"

He turned away again, facing the open window. "That, and it's taken most of my savings to keep the bar afloat," he said quietly, almost reluctantly. After what he'd just told her about his childhood, she supposed Cooper, a loner for the most part, wasn't used to sharing his feelings or thoughts with anyone.

"Why not just let it close? Obviously your uncle doesn't worry about it, so why should you?"

He spun around to face her, the sharp angles of his handsome face suddenly hard and unyielding. "Because The Wilde Side is all Hayden knows. It's all he has."

"He certainly doesn't seem too concerned about it if he's—what did you call it?—chasing skirt."

"I owe him, Carly. He raised me after my mom died, and I wasn't an easy kid to raise. I'll find a way to keep the bar open and hopefully start making a profit so it can run in the black. If I'm real lucky, it'll repay me the money I've put into it the past six months."

He stalked out of the bedroom. Carly considered leaving him alone, but she couldn't ignore the hint of pain that flashed in his eyes and filled his voice, or how her heart twisted with the knowledge. She shouldn't care, but she did. She had her own life to rebuild without worrying about a stranger's, but that didn't stop her from following Cooper into the living room.

"You need customers," she said when she found him folding the newspaper she'd left open on the coffee table.

He looked up, giving her another one of those tolerant looks. "Gee, you think?"

She stuffed her hands in the back pockets of her jeans. "Don't be sarcastic, Coop. I think I know how you can get a few."

"What do you know about running a bar?" He picked up the newspaper and carried it into the kitchen. "You're barely old enough to be allowed inside one."

She chose to ignore the truth behind that statement, and blurted, "I have a proposition for you." She was venturing into treacherous territory, but if she could help Cooper, and herself in the bargain, she was more than willing to take a few risks.

He set the newspaper in a box marked Recycle and looked at her. A slow grin eased across his lips, and the look he gave her was nothing short of wicked.

She struggled past the heated look and how her heart skipped about a half dozen beats in response. "I need my own apartment," she said, unwilling to give up now that the idea had taken hold. "Until I can find a job that doesn't require me to take off my clothes, I can't afford it."

His hands shot to his hips and he glared down at her. "What do you mean, take off your clothes?" he demanded.

"I'm a dancer, Cooper. At least that's what I'm trained to do. The only jobs in the paper that come even remotely close are for places like Wally's World of Women or Sahara Sam's, and that's not the kind of employment I envision putting on my résumé."

"You could always go home," he said, the glare still firmly in place.

"No," she said, shaking her head. "I'm going to make it on my own and do things my way for once in my life. What would you say if I looked for a job during the day, and at night, helped out at the bar and worked at finding a way to increase your customer base. If, by the end of two weeks, I haven't done that, then I'll be gone."

"You want to stay here for two weeks?"

She hid a smile at the disbelief tingeing his voice. "Where else am I going to stay? I'm short of cash and I still don't know what's wrong with my car. You get someone to share the cooking and cleaning, and I get a place to live while I look for a decent job in exchange for customer relations. Sounds like a great plan to me."

"Sounds like a disaster to me," he groused, and walked past her. "No."

She followed him into the living room. "Cooper, be

reasonable. It's a great solution to both of our problems."

He spun around, leveling his intense gaze on her. "It'd be the start of a whole new set of problems. We can't live together."

"We wouldn't be living together," she attempted to reason. "Not in the living-in-sin sense. We'd be more like roommates than anything else."

He continued to look at her as if she'd lost every ounce of common sense she possessed. Maybe she had, but in her opinion, her proposition was a perfect solution. He needed help with the bar, and she needed a place to live until she found a job.

"Princess, we both know if you stay here, you'll be sharing my bed by the end of the week."

She bit her lip. There was little doubt about the truth of that statement. They'd known each other only two days and already the chemical reaction was close to explosive. She couldn't look at Cooper without thinking of all sorts of interesting ways she'd love to explore that finely honed body. Although she might not be the most worldly and sophisticated of women, she knew lust in a man's eyes when she saw it—and Cooper's repeated glances in her direction were more often than not filled with desire.

She pulled her hands from her pockets and crossed her arms. Turning her head slightly to the side, she gave him a smile she hoped was inviting. "I really don't think that would be such a bad thing."

He blew out a stream of breath filled with frustration. "That's because you obviously don't know right from wrong."

Her smile widened. "My father was a minister,

Coop. I grew up knowing so much about right and wrong it's instinctual now."

"Then you must've slept through his sermons on sins of the flesh," he said, shoving a hand through his hair, then rubbing at the back of his neck.

She closed the distance between them and looked up into his horrified gaze. Using the tip of her finger, she traced a circle on the center of his chest. "Quite the contrary, Cooper," she said in her sultriest voice. "But I did learn a long time ago that Daddy wasn't always right about everything"

8

Rule 8: A lady should never concern herself with financial matters, as such things are better left to gentlemen.

UNFORTUNATELY, at least in Carly's opinion, Cooper couldn't have been more wrong. By Thursday evening, the closest she'd come to being anywhere near his bed was to set a stack of T-shirts she'd folded on his dresser after she'd done a couple loads of laundry. Of course, that didn't mean she hadn't thought about Cooper and his big bed a whole lot. The power of suggestion was indeed effective.

As usual, little activity filled the bar. The jukebox played the same old tunes popular in another decade. The same half dozen or so regulars lined up on bar stools shooting the breeze with one another or simply drinking quietly, with their own thoughts for company. Two hours ago Cooper had disappeared into the back office, leaving her and Karen alone to see to the actual running of the bar. Not that it took much effort considering the low-profile clientele nursing their beers tonight. She almost wished Benny and Joe would show up. She hadn't seen them since the night she'd wandered into the bar looking for a telephone. At least their presence would no doubt liven the place up a bit.

Carly made change for Marty, who challenged Fred to a game of pool then moved back to the stool behind the counter. This was the second night in a row she'd worked with Karen. The conversation wasn't only entertaining, thanks to Karen's dry sense of humor, but also quite enlightening. According to the long-time waitress, The Wilde Side had been on a downhill slide for the past couple of years, and the decline had nothing to do with Cooper's management. In fact, since Cooper had taken over for his disappearing uncle, business had actually increased.

By what? Carly wondered. Three customers?

"What've you been reading all night?" Karen asked her after serving a fresh round of drinks down at the far end of the bar.

Carly marked her page and held up the marketing and management book she'd checked out of the public library earlier that day when she'd dropped a postcard to her parents in the mail. She hadn't divulged her location, but she did at least let them know she was doing well and would contact them soon. It hadn't been much by way of information, but at least they'd know she was alive.

"Not that it's given me any ideas," she complained to Karen. She'd promised Cooper she'd find a way to increase business, but so far, all she'd read consisted of theory and nothing whatsoever to do with practice. Her journey on the job front had been equally disappointing. There wasn't a choreographer in the theater district hiring, and she'd left her résumé with every single one of them. She wasn't looking to get on stage, but to hopefully land a job as an assistant choreographer, or even an assistant to an assistant. So far, no one had called, and after three days, she was beginning to lose hope. She had to face reality. Since taking off her clothes at Wally's World of Women wasn't an option, if by the end of two weeks she didn't have *respectable* employment, she'd have no choice but to return to Homer and take the teaching job waiting for her.

"I should've checked out a book on tulips," she muttered.

"What are you talking about?" Karen asked.

"Nothing," Carly said with a wave of her hand.

Karen pulled up the other stool and sat, her dark eyes inquisitive. "You studying for something?"

Carly sighed. "I'm trying to come up with a way to generate some business around this place."

"Good luck," Karen said with a chuckle. "About the only thing that might bring a crowd into this place would be if we put in a stage and advertised half-naked women. I don't think Hayden would appreciate coming home to find out The Wilde Side had gone quite that wild."

Carly grinned. She'd gotten used to Karen's abrupt sense of humor. "If you were going to go out to a bar, would you bother to come here?"

"No," Karen answered. "But I work here, remember?"

Carly shook her head. "Say you didn't work here. Would The Wilde Side be a place you'd come to for a night of fun?"

"You're kidding, right?"

"Dead serious." Carly folded her arms. "So, would you?"

"Not in a pig's eye," Karen said stoically.

Carly sighed. That's what she was afraid of. "Why?" she asked. "What is it about this place that turns people off?"

"Take a look around, Carly," Karen said with a

sweep of her hand in a grand gesture. "This place is a dump."

"Say we cleaned it up a bit. Then would you come here for a good time?"

"Probably not." Karen shrugged and slid off the bar stool. "Sorry, Carly. But if I'm going to go out, I want to at least go where I can flirt with a doll-baby or two instead of these cranky old codgers."

"I resemble that remark," a gray-haired, weathered-faced man called out from halfway down the bar.

"And here I thought the reason you kept coming back was to win my heart," another regular on Carly's left added.

"Your broken-down old heart's already taken, Ernie." Karen slid a fresh beer in front of him. "Or do you need me to call your wife and have her remind you?"

"Ah now," Ernie hung his head sheepishly. "Don't you go gettin' her all in a huff."

"Then you'd better behave yourself," Karen said in a teasing, but chastising, tone.

Karen moved down the bar to serve more drinks and exchange a few good-humored comments with the guys, leaving Carly alone with her book.

That's what The Wilde Side needed, she thought. A draw. Something that would bring them in and keep them coming back for more.

She glanced around the bar. The joint sure could use a face-lift, but since they were operating in the red, a complete interior overhaul was out of the question. If she asked him, she'd bet Cooper would be willing to spring for some paint at the very least. And updated selections in the jukebox were a must. There wasn't a Top Forty hit or so much as a snappy country number to be had. Pink Floyd, The Rolling Stones and Creedence Clearwater Revival didn't produce many dance tunes.

Dance tunes? Dancing?

Why not? She set her book down with a snap and looked at the older crowd. These were blue-collar men. Men who worked with their hands for a living. If what she was thinking worked, she could very well alienate the men who depended on The Wilde Side as their main source of recreation. Unless she limited her plan to one night a week. It'd be a start, and if she succeeded, that one night four times a month would keep the bar open, repay Cooper and maybe even allow the place to see a decent profit for a change.

Carly slipped off the bar stool and slid out from behind the bar to follow Karen, who was busy cleaning up a recently deserted table. "What would bring in those doll-babies you were talking about?"

Karen continued to wipe down the table. "If you need to ask," she said, her voice infused with humor, "then you are young."

"Could you be serious for a minute, please?"

Karen straightened and looked at Carly. "Well..." she said, her expression thoughtful. "Women, I suppose."

"That's what I thought."

"You lost me, Cassidy."

"If we want business to pick up, we need something to draw them in and keep them coming back."

Karen picked up the tray with the empty glasses and headed back toward the bar. "That's pretty much a no-brainer."

Carly followed her. "How about something along the lines of ladies' night?" she asked as Karen set the dirty glasses in the tub of soapy water.

"Ladies' night?"

"Yeah. Ladies' night." Why hadn't she thought of this sooner? Her plan was perfect and darned near foolproof, with one little exception. "Entice them with inexpensive drinks, provide a little entertainment, and we'll have standing room only," she explained. "We get the women in here, and then men will surely follow. Business picks up and everybody's happy."

Karen's eyes narrowed with suspicion. "What kind of entertainment?"

Carly flashed her new friend a wide grin. "You just leave that to me," she said, then headed toward the office to spring her plan on Cooper.

COOPER CLOSED the ledger and looked up at Carly as if she'd lost her mind. "Ladies' night? At The Wilde Side?" he asked incredulously.

She braced her hands on the edge of his desk. She wore a scoop-necked top, and he struggled to keep his gaze locked with hers, since it was drawn to the red cotton neckline like a bull to a matador's cape. If he wasn't careful, he'd start snorting and stomping his foot.

The past few days had been miserable. His body wouldn't let him forget for a second that he wanted Carly. Only his conscience kept him from following through on the demands of his body. She'd only be a part of his life for two weeks. If she didn't find a job, she'd be heading back to whatever small town she'd escaped from. If by chance she did find a job, and with her unique qualifications he had serious doubts on that score, she'd be moving out of his place. Once his uncle returned, his plans didn't include sticking around Chicago. Any affair they did have would be brief.

He had a bad feeling his obsession ran beyond brief.

"Why is that so hard to imagine?" she countered, not the least bit offended by his response to her unwelcome suggestion.

He leaned back in the chair and folded his hands over his abdomen, concentrating on their conversation and not the way her eyes flashed with color or how her voluptuous curves teased him to the point of distraction. "You've been working in the bar for exactly five days. And how many women have you served?"

She straightened and folded her arms beneath her breasts.

Toro! Toro!

He resisted the ridiculous urge to stomp his foot.

"Well, none," she said with a lift of one shoulder. "But that's my whole point. You have to get women to come to The Wilde Side. Once you get them, then you'll attract the men. Before you know it, you'll have more than enough customers to keep the bar running on its own and even recoup the money you've had to put into it."

Surprisingly, Cooper thought, she did have a point. A very valid one he couldn't completely ignore.

"Ladies' night, huh?" he murmured, turning the idea over in his mind. What would it take? He'd have to make a few of those frozen concoctions women generally preferred, but he'd grown up learning how to mix drinks. Daiquiris, piña coladas and Singapore slings weren't all that tough to handle. "You think a weekly drink special would help?" he suggested.

"Most definitely," she agreed, flashing him a bright grin that filled her turquoise eyes with joy. "And I'd like to see about painting the interior. It's so dingy and

We'd like to send you **2 FREE** novels and a surprise gift to introduce you to Harlequin Temptation®. Accept our special offer today and

Indulge in a Harlequin Moment!

HOW TO QUALIFY:

1. With a coin, carefully scratch off the silver area on the card at right to see what we have for you—**2 FREE BOOKS** and a **FREE GIFT**—**ALL YOURS! ALL FREE!**

2. Send back the card and you'll receive two brand-new Harlequin Temptation® novels. These books have a cover price of $3.99 each in the U.S. and $4.50 each in Canada, but they are yours to keep absolutely free!

3. There's no catch. You're under no obligation to buy anything. We charge nothing—ZERO—for your first shipment and you don't have to make any minimum number of purchases—not even one!

4. The fact is, thousands of readers enjoy receiving books by mail from the Harlequin Reader Service®. They enjoy the convenience of home delivery… they like getting the best new novels at discount prices, BEFORE they're available in stores…and they love their *Heart to Heart* subscriber newsletter featuring author news, horoscopes, recipes, book reviews and much more!

5. We hope that after receiving your free books you'll want to remain a subscriber. But the choice is yours—to continue or cancel, any time at all. So why not take us up on our invitation with no risk of any kind. You'll be glad you did!

SPECIAL FREE GIFT!

We can't tell you what it is…but we're sure you'll like it! A FREE gift just for giving the Harlequin Reader Service® a try!

Visit us online at
www.eHarlequin.com

The **2 FREE BOOKS** we send you will be selected from **HARLEQUIN TEMPTATION®**, the series that brings you sexy, sizzling and seductive stories.

Books received may vary.

Scratch off the silver area to see what the Harlequin Reader Service has for you.

HARLEQUIN®
Makes any time special™

YES! I have scratched off the silver area above. Please send me the **2 FREE** books and gift for which I qualify. I understand I am under no obligation to purchase any books, as explained on the back and on the opposite page.

NAME   (PLEASE PRINT CLEARLY)

ADDRESS

APT.#   CITY

STATE/ PROV.   ZIP/POSTAL CODE

342 HDL C4HN

142 HDL C4HE
(H-T-OS-09/00)

THE HARLEQUIN READER SERVICE® —Here's how it works:

Accepting your 2 free books and gift places you under no obligation to buy anything. You may keep the books and gift and return the shipping statement marked "cancel." If you do not cancel, about a month later we'll send you 4 additional novels and bill you just $3.34 each in the U.S., or $3.80 each in Canada, plus 25¢ shipping & handling per book and applicable taxes if any.* That's the complete price and — compared to cover prices of $3.99 each in the U.S. and $4.50 each in Canada — it's quite a bargain! You may cancel at any time, but if you choose to continue, every month we'll send you 4 more books, which you may either purchase at the discount price or return to us and cancel your subscription.

*Terms and prices subject to change without notice. Sales tax applicable in N.Y. Canadian residents will be charged applicable provincial taxes and GST.

BUSINESS REPLY MAIL
FIRST-CLASS MAIL   PERMIT NO. 717   BUFFALO, NY

POSTAGE WILL BE PAID BY ADDRESSEE

HARLEQUIN READER SERVICE
3010 WALDEN AVE
PO BOX 1867
BUFFALO NY 14240-9952

NO POSTAGE
NECESSARY
IF MAILED
IN THE
UNITED STATES

If offer card is missing write to: Harlequin Reader Service, 3010 Walden Ave., P.O. Box 1867, Buffalo NY 14240-1867

DETACH AND MAIL CARD TODAY!

really could use a fresh coat of paint to brighten it up a little."

Another expense he really couldn't afford, but she was right again. If the goal was to increase business, they didn't want potential new customers turned off by the shabbiness of the bar. "I'll see about the paint," he reluctantly agreed. "But you don't want bright in a bar, Carly. Subdued is more what you're looking for."

"Subdued," she agreed, "and maybe even some softer lighting. If our goal is to attract female clientele, we don't want harsh lighting, either."

"What does lighting have to do with anything?"

She moved suddenly and propped her denim-clad hip on the edge of the cluttered desk. "You ever notice how in department stores the lighting in dressing rooms and at the makeup counters is different than the rest of the store?"

"Not really."

She fiddled with a sheaf of papers stacked in the tray on the corner of the desk. "Well, it is," she said, disrupting the neatness of the papers with a flick of her finger. "And it's because the softer lighting makes us feel better about the way we look. If we feel good about that, then we're more confident. And if we're confident, we'll interact more openly with the opposite sex. It's basic psychology, Cooper."

The thought of Carly interacting with anyone of the opposite sex besides him had his insides twisting. He couldn't be jealous. Not Cooper Wilde, the quintessential loner.

"You have this all figured out, don't you?" he asked rhetorically.

She fanned the papers in the tray and shrugged. "You won't be sorry, Coop. I promise."

He expected her to leave, but she didn't. She just sat there on the edge of the desk, looking down at him, her bottom lip trapped between her teeth. "Something else on your mind, Carly?"

There was a lot on his mind, but very little of it had to do with increasing business—it was all about increasing his libido. And he laid the blame solely at the sexy little feet of the distracting platinum blonde with more guts than common sense, who was twisting him in knots and messing up his paperwork.

"Well," she finally said, "it really is slow out there tonight. Would you mind terribly if Karen and I took off for the rest of the evening? I want to do more research on this ladies' night idea, and since I don't know the city all that well, I'd rather not go alone."

"I'll go. Karen can watch the bar."

She shook her head and stood. "Thanks, but, uh—" she inched toward the door "—if it's not a problem, I'd really rather take Karen. It *is* ladies' night we're after, and uh...her opinion would be more accurate than yours. You know, you being a man and all."

Cooper shrugged as if her rejection didn't affect him in the least. Quite the contrary. A night alone with Carly away from the bar held a whole lot of appeal. "Sure. Go ahead," he said, then opened the ledger again. "I'll be out in a minute."

The grin she'd graced him with before she slipped out the door was filled with relief.

And that made him nervous as hell.

"SO THIS IS YOUR idea of entertainment," Karen said, looking around the nightclub with interest and loads of feminine pleasure in eyes. "Does Cooper know what you're planning?"

"I didn't exactly tell him every little detail of my plan," Carly admitted, sidling up to the crowded bar beside Karen. "But it's going to work and he'll have no reason to object. Even if he does end up eighty-sixing the idea after one night, I'll still have accomplished what I set out to."

"You can't be serious? He'll be livid when he finds out," Karen warned.

Carly took a sip of the rum and cola she'd ordered when they first arrived at the popular exotic male dancer nightclub. "This is going to work, and he'll be too busy counting the money in the till to be mad."

Country music blared from the speakers as the next dancer took the stage. Carly eased onto a vacant bar stool and stared mesmerized as a barefoot cowboy wearing chaps and a pearl-studded western shirt slowly ground his hips in time to the slow beat of the music. The music changed suddenly to an upbeat rockabilly tune. She nearly choked on her drink when the sandy-blond cowboy pulled the chaps from his body with a quick jerk. The shirt followed, leaving him wearing nothing but a leather G-string and a wicked smile.

"Sweet Mary," she muttered, when a customer dressed in a prim suit looped a folded bill into the cowboy's G-string.

"You'd better get a grip," Karen said over the music and the shouts of encouragement from the all-female crowd. "Especially since you plan to turn The Wilde Side into something this wild and crazy."

"I think we'll go with a little classier routine," she said, then downed the rest of her drink. "No complete stripping."

"Oh, that'll work," Karen said, then gave a whoop of encouragement to the gyrating cowboy.

The dancer left the stage, and the swirling lights dimmed to nearly black. Carly strained to see what was happening and caught a movement. She waited with the few hundred women to see what kind of entertainment was next. A spotlight shone in the far corner of the stage. Two men in black briefs carried a coffin out, their oiled muscles straining and bulging from the weight. If they weren't enough to have the women shouting and screaming for more, they stood the casket on end, clicked the latch then quietly left the stage.

The music swelled—an eerie, haunting melody—and then the lid of the casket slowly opened to reveal a dancer dressed as a vampire.

"Oh my God," Karen said. "He's gorgeous!"

Carly sniffed. She supposed he could be considered somewhat good-looking, if a girl went for the skinny but muscular type. She preferred them with a little more meat on them.

Like Cooper.

And certainly with a wider chest that tapered into lean hips.

Like Cooper, her conscience taunted again.

Most definitely like Cooper, she thought, signaling the bartender for another drink. She watched the vampire dancer move around the stage, swaying his hips and giving the ladies a teasing glimpse of his black-leather-clad backside, and was staunchly unimpressed when he tugged the leather from his behind and actually wiggled it at the crowd.

Carly rolled her eyes. Cooper's butt was much cuter.

"I've seen enough," she said to Karen. "Are you going to give me a hand finding the hired help or do I have to do this alone?"

Karen reluctantly tore her gaze from the shimmying vampire. "I'll help, I'll help," she said, her voice filled with humor. "This could actually be a lot of fun."

Carly paid the bartender for another round of drinks after she showed him her ID, *again*, then shifted on the stool to scan the shirtless waiters of the popular nightclub.

"What about him?" Karen suggested, pointing the mouth of her bottle of light beer toward a tall waiter with shoulders wider than a Chicago Bear linebacker.

Carly sipped her drink. "He has potential," she agreed.

Karen fanned herself dramatically. "He has a lot more than potential."

"I guess we'd better get started." Carly downed a hefty portion of rum and cola before waving over the waiter.

He had light brown hair, clear green eyes and a smooth, hairless chest that tapered to a washboard belly. The waiters all wore tight satin slacks that left very little to the imagination. He leaned toward Carly. "What can I get you, ladies?"

"About two hours of your time," Carly blurted.

The waiter straightened and frowned. "Excuse me?"

She sighed. All beauty and no brains, she thought. "Do you dance?" she asked slowly, just in case he didn't understand her.

His frown deepened. "You want a drink or not, lady?"

Carly looked at Karen and rolled her eyes at her friend's knowing smirk. "This isn't going to be as easy I thought it would."

"Watch and learn, Cassidy," Karen said saucily, then laid her hand on the waiter's forearm.

"What's your name, honey?" she asked him in the same saucy tone filled with more confidence than Carly ever hoped to possess. Maybe if she did, she would be in Cooper's bed by now.

"Ken," the waiter answered.

"What my friend was trying to ask is whether or not you'd be interested in a job. A hundred and fifty bucks for about ten minutes work."

That got his attention, and he stopped looking at Carly as if she'd lost her mind. "What's the catch?"

"No catch," Carly offered. "It's a perfectly legitimate job offer. And it's legal, too."

"What's the job?" the Ken doll asked carefully.

"Being a dancer for ladies' night at The Wilde Side," Karen told him. "Two sets and you make easy money."

"Thanks for the offer, but I'm not a professional. You want one of those guys," he said, jerking his thumb in the direction of the pirate who'd taken the stage.

Those guys were too expensive and Carly knew it. "Can you dance?" she asked him.

"I can hold my own on the dance floor."

"If you've got rhythm, then I can teach you how to dance like them."

He shook his head, his bottle-green eyes filling with a reluctance that nearly had Carly upping her price. She couldn't afford to go any higher than she'd already offered, since she had ten dancers to hire for the night.

"I don't know...."

"There'll be absolutely nothing sleazy about our dancers," Carly said, borrowing a little of Karen's confidence. "I promise. Just take off your shirt, dance for the ladies and maybe flirt a little. From what I've been seeing here tonight, it looks like the tips are great. You could probably make an extra fifty to a hundred bucks on top of what we'll pay you."

Carly scribbled the address on a napkin and handed it to the waiter. "Be there at noon Saturday. And if you have a couple of friends that might be interested, bring them along."

The waiter smiled at them and nodded. "I'll see what I can do."

Karen turned toward Carly and lifted her bottle of beer for a toast. "We did it," she said, then laughed. "I can't believe it, but we actually did it."

"One down," Carly said, touching her glass to Karen's. "And nine more to go."

9

Rule 9: A lady will never be out after sunset unless she has a male escort.

CARLY FOLLOWED Karen through the entrance of the all-night restaurant, squinting under the glare of the fluorescent lights. "What are we doing here?"

"Sobering you up before I take you home to Coop," Karen muttered, and signaled the waitress for a table for two.

Carly let out a sigh and hurried after Karen and the waitress. "I'm not drunk. Just—" she slid into the plum vinyl booth opposite Karen "—just a little tipsy, is all."

Karen turned their coffee mugs right side up and took the menus the waitress offered. "And you had how many rum and cokes tonight?"

Carly waited for the waitress to fill her cup with steaming coffee, then lifted it to her lips and sipped carefully. Probably more than she should have, she realized, attempting to focus on her coffee. Five days ago, she'd had her first drink and had gotten so inebriated she'd not only done the unthinkable by passing out cold in the bathroom of The Wilde Side, but she'd woken up in a strange man's apartment. Of course, she couldn't very well curse her poor judgment when it meant she'd met the one man who managed to make her forget about rules and start thinking about all things forbidden.

Except she couldn't seem to get him to do anything but kiss her, she thought with a frown, flipping open the glossy menu. They'd been so close to something much more interesting the day Karen had interrupted them in the storage room, but since Cooper's parting remark about virginity, he hadn't so much as hinted that he wanted to make love to her.

She snapped the menu closed. There had to be something inherently wrong with the man. He wanted her. She knew he did, so why hadn't he done anything about it? It wasn't as if she hadn't let him know she wanted him, too.

After giving their order to the waitress, Carly finished her coffee, then signaled for another. "How long have you known Cooper?" she asked Karen.

Karen thanked the waitress for the coffee, then added creamer to her mug. "About five years, I guess."

Carly propped her chin in her hand. "I've only known him five days."

"So I've heard," Karen said dryly.

Carly frowned. "You know, an awful lot can happen in just five days."

"Such as?" Karen set her spoon on the napkin and sipped her coffee.

"Like getting all tingly and stuff."

Karen laughed suddenly. "Tingly? And stuff?"

"Uh-huh," Carly said with a nod.

"I keep forgetting how young you really are. What's with all this tingly stuff? Just say it, Carly," Karen said in a straightforward manner that Carly appreciated, and wished she could emulate. "Cooper makes you hot."

Carly let out a long, gusty sigh. "Does he ever," she admitted. Hot. Inferno hot.

"You gonna do something about it?" Karen asked her.

"I dunno," Carly answered with a shrug. "I want to."

Karen leaned forward, clasping her hands loosely around the mug. "Then what's stopping you?"

Carly couldn't answer. Cooper was stopping her, she supposed. All those mixed signals weren't only frustrating, but darned hard to decipher.

Karen let out a sigh filled with exasperation. "If no one can get hurt, then where's the harm?"

Carly sat up straighter and looked at Karen. She did have a point. There was no one special in her life any longer. Cooper wasn't seeing anyone, either. What was wrong with two people enjoying each other's bodies? "You're right, I suppose," she said slowly.

Karen shrugged. "Then why not? Coop wants you. You want him. There's nothing wrong with that."

"But..."

"But what?" Karen interrupted before Carly could argue.

Carly bit her bottom lip. For as much as she was determined to break all those confining rules of her childhood and establish her own laws to live by, she didn't believe she was sophisticated enough to make love to a man then casually walk away with her heart intact. Too many years of training prevented her from adopting such a cavalier attitude about sex. Just because she wanted to live her life her way and not by the dictates of another, didn't mean she'd lost all of her scruples. Making love had to mean something other than just a fun time to be had by the parties involved. Didn't it?

One thing she didn't have any doubts about—if Cooper made love the way he kissed, Carly was dead certain they'd have more than just fun. "What if someone got hurt?" she asked eventually.

Disbelief filled Karen's clear, dark eyes. "You're falling for Coop, aren't you?"

Carly gasped. "Of course not. That's—" not too far fetched "—that's silly."

"Then tell Coop you want him. Or would you rather spend the rest of your life wondering what if?"

Carly grinned. *What if* had gotten her this far.

The only problem she could find with Karen's advice was, even if she and Cooper did make love, there'd be a whole new set of what if's. Particularly the big, *what if* she fell in love with him when there was no chance of them ever having a relationship beyond the bedroom?

FEELING MUCH more like herself by the time Karen dropped her off outside Cooper's apartment, Carly quietly crept up the back stairs, careful not to make too much noise. Especially since it was after four in the morning.

All in all, the night had been a success. Not only had she and Karen managed to hire ten "doll-babies" as dancers, but she'd also gleaned some valuable and practical advice from her new friend during the two hours they'd sat and talked in the restaurant. Particularly advice on how to handle men. One man especially.

Carly's Law: Life's too short for what if's.

Now she just needed the confidence to back up that law. A solid plan that would make Cooper forget about his silly code of honor and stop denying the special blend of magic happening between them. Exactly how she planned to accomplish this feat, she hadn't decided.

She let herself into the apartment and locked the door behind her. A smile tipped her lips upward. He'd left a light burning for her, a gesture that, while simple, made her smile just the same. After turning off the lamp, she crept into the hallway toward her bedroom. She flipped on the light and gasped in surprise at the very large male sitting on the edge of the small twin bed.

"Where have you been?" he demanded, coming off the bed toward her.

Carly bristled at the tone of his voice. Just who did he think he was? "With Karen," she answered. "We were conducting research."

His thick, corded arms crossed over his wide chest. "Exactly what kind research keeps you out until four in the morning?"

She let out a sigh and stepped around him. She wasn't used to being interrogated and didn't like it one bit. Of course, she'd never done anything in her life that required an interrogation. "We stopped to have breakfast and sat and talked for a while."

"Until 4:00 a.m.?" he questioned, his voice rising.

She tossed her satin bag on the bed and turned back to face him. "Well, gee, Cooper," she said, planting her hands on her hips. "You know how women are. When we're gossiping everything else just flies right out of our pretty, empty little heads and we lose track of all the important things. Like time."

"There's no reason to get sarcastic."

"And you," she said, taking the two steps necessary to stand directly in front of him and poke him in the chest with her index finger, "have no right to question me. What I do is my business, Wilde."

"If you're living here, then I have every right."

"Wanna bet?"

He snagged her wrist before she could drill his chest again. "I was worried," he said, his dark brown eyes softening with an emotion that made her throat instantly tighten. She didn't believe for a minute she saw love lining his gaze, but he cared, and for now, that was enough to give her just enough confidence to follow Karen's sage advice about the opposite sex.

"You were?" she asked in a hushed whisper.

He smoothed his thumb over her wrist, causing gooseflesh to prickle her skin, and nodded. "Chicago can be a pretty nasty place."

"I was perfectly safe."

"I still worried," he countered. He tugged on her wrist, pulling her even closer, so their bodies were touching.

She breathed in his scent, an intricate blend of aftershave and male.

Of Cooper.

Tipping her head back, she held her breath as he angled his head. She waited as he slowly brought his mouth down to hers, trembled when he nipped gently at her bottom lip, then moaned softly when he traced his tongue over the spot. His mouth finally slipped over hers and heat exploded around them.

She wound her arms around his neck. This is what she wanted. This and more that Cooper continued to keep out of her reach. Something wonderful and spontaneous. Magical and impulsive. Hot and exciting.

She wanted Cooper.

He lifted his head to look down at her. Desire filled

his eyes along with that other, more heady emotion she could only describe as caring.

"You're bad news," he said roughly, then slipped one hand along her jaw and into her hair. He cupped the back of her head in his big hand, and before she could blink, he captured her mouth again in a kiss so deep and wet she trembled in his arms.

From the reverence banked in his gaze, she expected him to go slow and easy. She expected gentleness, tenderness. Instead he produced enough heat to reduce her to ash.

His tongue slid across hers. He tasted a little like peppermint, and a whole lot like man. Tiny shivers of delight rippled through her as he teased her mouth, demanding a response she willingly gave. Her nipples beaded against the satin of her bra, the sensation adding to the heat Cooper so effortlessly fanned into a three-alarm, blazing inferno.

His other hand moved from her back, coming to rest on her hip. Even through the denim of her jeans, she could feel his touch pressing into her soft flesh. He rocked her closer, his powerful legs grazing against her thighs, sending another spiral of heat through her, this one settling low in her tummy and winding its way down to where she ached to have him inside her.

The hand holding her head moved, his fingertips teasing her jaw, then tracing lazy patterns down her throat, until he finally brushed the swell of her breasts. His thumb rhythmically smoothed along the topside of her bra, dipping lower to tease her nipple into a taut, hard peak. She trembled again at the delicious sensations making her feel so very much alive.

The fingers teasing her breast moved to her shoulder, and he gently eased her away from him. He lifted his head, and she looked into his eyes, feeling a wealth of pleasure ribbon through her at the heat lingering in his gaze.

Maybe Karen was right, after all. No one could get hurt unless she was silly enough to lose her heart to a guy like Cooper. An intrinsic loner who claimed he didn't need anyone in his life, least of all a woman to complicate things and, heaven forbid, distract him. If she did lose her heart, she'd have no one to blame but herself. Even after only five days, they obviously cared about each other. But was it really enough for her to make love to Cooper? Regardless of her claims of living life her way, did she really have it in her to make love and then walk away?

There was only one way to find out.

"Make love to me, Cooper," she whispered.

To his credit, he didn't look the least bit surprised by her sensual demand. Slowly, he pulled her arms from his neck. "Carly..."

"How can you honestly deny this is something we both want?"

He massaged the back of his neck and looked toward the ceiling. Finding no answer, he blew out a ragged stream of breath before bringing his gaze back to hers. "I can't, Carly," he said, regret tingeing his deep, smooth voice.

"Can't what? Make love to me? Or deny that you want me as much as I want you?"

"What do you want from me?"

She closed the distance he was intent on putting between them. "You, Cooper," she said quietly, sliding her hand over his chest, stopping at the heavy pounding of his heart. "I want you."

Cooper couldn't move. She'd cast some crazy kind of

spell on him and his limbs refused to cooperate with the signals and alarms going off in his head to get the hell out of her room. Fast, before he did something really stupid, like take her up on her very generous and tempting offer.

He couldn't. He couldn't make love to Carly and not follow in the same pattern as the rest of the Wildes. He'd make love to her, then that's all he'd think about. When she wised up and returned to that big family of hers, he'd end up just like Hayden and his mom had, nursing a broken heart and mooning pathetically over the one who'd torn it out of his chest and stomped all over it.

No way.

Not Cooper Wilde.

He muttered something profane and pulled Carly against him. No man alive had enough willpower to resist her. Especially not one physically incapable of fighting genetics. He dipped his head and slanted his mouth over hers in a kiss so hot and erotic he didn't have time to think about defective genes. The only jeans he had any interest in were the ones he wanted her out of so desperately.

She stretched up on her tiptoes and wrapped her arms around his neck, crushing her full breasts against his chest. She wiggled, brushing them back and forth, heightening his awareness to the point of pain. The woman was tempting him beyond belief.

A painful groan ripped from his chest. He moved them toward the small twin bed and gently eased them down to the mattress. The bed squeaked, the box spring protesting under his added weight. He didn't care. Let the damn thing break, so long as he got to feel her beneath him.

He lifted his head and searched her face, hesitating, looking for any sign, however remote, that she didn't want what was happening between them. All he found was need and desire.

Another groan ripped from his chest in painful surrender, and then he captured her mouth in a sizzling kiss she returned with the same hunger that was driving him. He tried to shift his weight, but the pressure behind his fly was nearly unbearable. He couldn't remember when he'd ever needed like this, ever wanted like this, ever felt so close to the edge like this.

God help him, only with Carly.

As frightened as that thought made him, he couldn't have stopped himself from skimming his hand over her denim-clad hip and beneath the hem of that distracting cotton top any more than he could stop something as monumental as world hunger. Some things in life were impossible, and controlling his need and desire for Carly was one of them.

Heaven help him, he needed. Needed Carly. Needed her and wanted her.

Bad.

He tore his mouth from hers and skimmed his tongue along her jaw and down her throat to the slope of her breasts, tasting her silky flesh. She moaned softly and arched toward his mouth and hands. His fingers found the front clasp of her satin bra and he freed her breasts, testing the heavy weight in his palm before pulling her tight pink nipple into his mouth.

She gasped and arched her back even more. Her fingers slid into his hair, holding him close.

As if he had any intention of going anywhere he couldn't touch or taste Carly.

A deep-rooted restlessness shifted through him. He

wanted to be inside her, wanted to brand her as his and stake his claim. If she knew what he was thinking, she'd no doubt call him a caveman again. Too bad, he thought. He wanted to make her his in every way a man could love a woman.

Making love to Carly would change everything, but he was dangerously close to beyond caring. She'd cast a spell over him, and he couldn't find the words to describe the strange connection between them any more than he could define his feelings for her.

She scared him, because she represented the very thing that could bring him to his knees. A distraction that could cost him his future if he let it, with him ending up as hopeless and pathetic as the rest of the Wildes.

Regardless of the fear, he still wanted her.

Losing himself in the magic could cost him, and he still wanted her.

He didn't believe for a minute that she was the one woman capable of making him believe in forever. Temporary. For as long as the fun lasted. He could do temporary. Temporary was his only hope of surviving.

Too bad Carly wasn't a temporary kind of woman.

His lifted his head and locked his gaze with hers. "This isn't supposed to happen," he said, smoothing his hand over her breast, down to her stomach, his fingers stopping at the fastening of her jeans.

"What's wrong with two people enjoying each other's bodies?" she asked him quietly. She slipped her hands beneath his T-shirt, smoothing her cool fingers over his back. She closed her eyes and arched toward him. "Touch me, Cooper," she whispered around a soft moan.

Each notch of the zipper he carefully pulled down

added to his final destruction. He pushed the heavy fabric first over one hip, then the other while she toed off her sneakers. He pulled the material from her legs and nearly came out of his skin when she slipped one smooth thigh between his legs.

His hand slid over her thigh, finally coming to a stop at the edge of a scrap of sinfully black satin. He skimmed his fingers over the smooth material, wondering somewhere in the back of his mind if he should stop them before they reached the point of no return.

He charged headlong into insanity, instead.

Heat and need intensified when he dipped his fingers beneath the satin edge. Desire exploded when he cupped her moist heat.

Carly's senses scattered in a thousand different directions. Her hips arched toward the honeyed stroke of Cooper's fingers intimately inside her. Her head spun. Her body coiled tight.

"Sweet Mary," she gasped in a breathless whisper. "I didn't know..."

"Let it go, Princess," he murmured, then slanted his mouth over hers, hot, open and wild. He stroked her body and mouth with a deep, slow, sensual rhythm that had her breath coming in short, hard gasps until finally, the tension coiled then exploded as she fell apart in his arms.

Tiny tremors shook her body as cognizance slowly returned. She tucked her face against Cooper's shoulder until the heavy pounding of her heart slowed to a more normal rhythm.

He pulled back to look down at her. Her already overworked heart slammed into ribs at the raw need in his eyes.

"If that was only the beginning," she told him, running her hands along the tension in his back, "I can't wait to see what you've got planned for the rest of the night."

Regret shoved need out the way. "I can't make love to you, Princess," he said, his voice rough and tight.

She stared at him, unable to believe what she'd just heard. Can't make love to her? "Why on earth not?" she blurted. "We've already established the fact that it'd be damned good. What's to stop us?"

"Ah, Princess. I do want you. So bad I ache. But I can't protect you."

She wasn't some helpless female needing protection. She needed him, in the most elemental way possible. "I don't need pro—" His meaning crept past her stung feminine pride. "Oh," she said. "*That* kind of protection."

He straightened what was left of her clothes and grinned sheepishly. "It's probably a discredit to my gender to admit this," he said, placing a light but firm kiss on her lips before easing away from her. "But I don't walk around with a condom in my wallet, or have a supply in my nightstand."

She smiled despite the loss of heat from his big body. She couldn't help herself. His honesty touched her deeply. That and the fact that he wasn't one of those jerks always on the prowl.

He stood and moved toward the door.

"That's it?" she asked, easing up on her elbows. "You're just going to go to sleep? Alone?"

He stopped and looked over his shoulder at her. Regret, need and that other emotion she couldn't define lined his handsome face. "Somehow, I don't think I'll be getting much sleep."

He walked out and left her alone, her body still humming from Cooper's delicious brand of lovemaking. She had a fleeting thought that perhaps she should be embarrassed by what had transpired between them, but how could she feel an ounce of shame over something so beautiful and exciting?

She let out a sigh, then readied herself for bed.

Alone.

A detail she planned to change. Pronto.

10

Rule 10: A lady should never question nor criticize a gentleman's decision.

COOPER SHOOK his head. Carly had left her mug and crumb-covered plate sitting in the sink before taking off to run a few errands. He placed the dishes in the dishwasher and set the switch, then walked into the living room. She'd surprised him by being up early considering it had been close to five in the morning before either one of them went to bed—alone.

Little good it'd done him, he thought crankily. He'd slept for maybe three hours, and they'd been anything but restful. Disturbing visions of a sexy platinum bombshell kept flitting through his dreams, making him ache for her even more.

On Fridays, Karen opened the bar, giving him most of the day to himself. He'd run his own errand shortly after Carly had left. No more excuses, he'd thought, as he'd walked into the drugstore down the block to purchase a box of condoms.

Making love to Carly was as close to insanity as he could get, but he supposed he was ready for a little craziness since he couldn't seem get her off his mind no matter how hard he tried. He'd been worried last night when she hadn't come home. He'd paced, he'd cursed and he'd even considered going to look for her except he hadn't a clue where she and Karen had gone. The relief that had coursed through him when she'd walked into the bedroom had spooked him. He cared. Something he hadn't planned or even wanted, but he couldn't change the fact that Carly Cassidy had gotten to him in ways he'd never dreamed possible.

Everywhere he looked lately, there was a reminder of her presence. If she didn't leave her sneakers in the living room where she kicked them off every night after they closed the bar, she left her dishes in the sink and not in the dishwasher, where they belonged. Obviously no one had ever taught her how to properly fold a newspaper after reading it, because every morning he'd find it folded carelessly on the coffee table. And if the woman ever learned how to replace a cap on a tube of toothpaste, he'd be shocked.

Carly was good at a lot of things. She had a way with the customers that surprised him, and could cook a mean pot roast, even if she did turn his kitchen into a disaster zone. But first and foremost she was a pro at messing up his orderly life. He liked things in their place. Carly lived in what she laughingly called organized clutter, which drove him crazy, and she rarely put anything back exactly the way she'd found it.

She drove him nuts in other ways, too. The way her perfume lingered long after she left a room, surrounding him and reminding him of what she could cost him if he let her. The sexy way her lips tipped into a grin made his heart beat frantically in his chest. The way she walked, talked and laughed, or how she looked at him when she thought he wasn't paying attention got to him in ways he hadn't expected. Everything about her disrupted his life.

He'd miss her when she left.

There hadn't been a single message from any of the prospective employers she'd contacted. In another week, she'd be gone. That was their deal. Two weeks. At the end of which she'd likely be on her way back to her family and the people who cared about her.

The front door opened and Carly burst into the living room, her arms loaded with packages. "You wouldn't believe the sales I found!"

He picked up the newspaper she'd left on the table and folded it neatly while she dropped her packages on the sofa and looked over her shoulder at him. "I didn't mean to go so crazy," she said, "but I did need a few things, and the sales were incredible. I've never shopped at a discount clothing warehouse before. Wanna see?"

Before he could answer, she started pulling items out of the bags. A couple pair of jeans, some shorts and a few tops along with something filmy and lacy.

"What do you think?" she asked, a wicked light shining in her eyes as she held up a turquoise scrap of satin that matched the color of her eyes. The black lace insert slashed across the front had his imagination kick starting all over again.

"You wouldn't believe the price I paid for this," she told him. "It was incredibly inexpensive."

She wouldn't believe the thoughts tripping through his mind. They were incredibly erotic.

"Well?" she prompted when he couldn't find his voice.

"Nice," he finally managed, and eased down into the recliner, the newspaper gripped tightly in his hand.

She flashed him a brilliant smile, then continued to dump more items from the bags. By the time she finished cluttering up the sofa and letting the bags fall to the floor, his living room was practically unrecognizable.

"Are you busy today?" she asked, sorting through the items she'd purchased.

Busy fantasizing. "Not really, why?" he said instead.

"I need to put these flyers up around the neighborhood. Wanna help?"

"Flyers?" he asked carefully. With Carly, he never quite knew what to expect.

She rummaged through the mess she had made. "Ah-ha! These flyers." She opened a box from a local printer and handed him a bright orange piece of paper. "I went to one of those printers that has computers for the customers to use, and made this. I thought we'd put them up around the neighborhood to advertise for ladies' night next Thursday. I was going to take an ad out in the *Sun Times*, but it's expensive. Five hundred flyers was less than twenty bucks."

He scanned the flyer advertising "A Walk on The Wilde Side for Ladies Only" along with her name and the phone number of the bar for more information or large party reservations. A line of small print at the bottom proclaimed gentlemen wouldn't be granted admittance until 10:00 p.m. When Carly had first approached him about ladies' night, he'd envisioned a weekly drink special, not closing the bar to men for a specific period of time. But Thursdays were generally slow, so what harm could there be in Carly's plan? Maybe it'd even work, but he seriously doubted they'd rake in the kind of money she anticipated.

After helping her carry her purchases into the bedroom, they left the apartment to saturate the neighborhood with flyers. The early afternoon sun was warm, but not unbearably hot, as he and Carly hung advertisements on telephone poles and asked the merchants in the neighborhood if they would place flyers in their shop windows. They even ventured farther away and strolled down Michigan Avenue before heading to the riverfront, where they stopped for lunch at an outdoor café of one of the hotels overlooking the river.

They placed their order with the waitress. Carly watched a series of water taxis and tourist boats skirt along the river. Cooper watched her.

"Oh, I forgot to check for messages before we left," she said suddenly, turning back to face him.

"There weren't any," he said, hating the disappointment that flared in her eyes.

She let out a sigh and propped her chin in her hands. "Oh well. A girl can hope, at least."

The waitress delivered their meal, then disappeared again. A light breeze fluttered the umbrella over their table as Carly bit enthusiastically into her cheeseburger.

He squirted ketchup on his plate, then sprinkled salt on his French fries. "You told me you were a dancer," he said, dragging a fry through the ketchup. "But you never did tell me what kind of job a dancer looks for."

She stirred the thick chocolate shake she'd ordered. "I'm hoping for something as an assistant choreographer. I'd even be a gopher at this stage. I just wish something would open up somewhere."

He already knew the answer, but he asked anyway. "What are you going to do if you don't find one? Go home?"

"I'll have to. After over three hundred bucks to fix my car and guaranteeing the..." She lowered her eyes suddenly and concentrated on adding pepper to her burger. "Let's just say my finances are depleting a lot more rapidly than I'd anticipated."

"I know the feeling," he muttered. "Let's hope your idea works."

Carly had decided that Karen was right and Cooper would no doubt be quite upset when he discovered exactly what her ladies' night entailed. She'd have to tell him eventually, but she'd rather wait until she had everything in place so it'd be impossible for him to renege.

"I think it will," she said, looking at him again. The navy blue T-shirt he wore stretched across his chest, and the fabric strained against his thick biceps. He wore a pair of aviator sunglasses against the harsh glare of the sunlight reflecting off the river, preventing her from seeing his eyes. She loved his eyes. They were so...intense.

"I'm hoping we make enough money so the bar can show a profit and you can get back the money you've put into it. Then, when your uncle comes home, you can start that business you want. Are you going to set it up here in Chicago?" she asked, trying to change the subject to something other than ladies' night. She wasn't exactly lying to him, she was just keeping certain information to herself until she was ready to let him in on her entire plan. She couldn't help wondering if her father would consider omission pushing the sin envelope just a bit too far.

"I was thinking about it," he said. "I'd be close to Hayden that way."

"But...?" she questioned. There was a hesitancy in his voice she couldn't help but notice. "I heard a 'but' in that statement."

He finished off his cheeseburger before he answered

her. "But," he said, pulling off his sunglasses, "I really like the east coast. I spent some time in New York when I was in the navy and liked it. It's not as hot as Chicago in the summer, and it doesn't snow half as much during the winter."

She'd known from the beginning there was no chance of a lasting relationship between them, but that didn't stop the disappointment she felt. What had she been hoping for? A declaration of undying love just because he'd managed to make her feel things she'd never felt with another man? Nothing said sex, no matter how great, equated to everlasting love.

"You'd move?" she asked. Her appetite waned suddenly. She set aside her cheeseburger and pushed the plate away. "All the way to New York? But your family is here."

"You gonna finish that?" he asked.

She shook her head, amazed that he could even think of food when her heart was so filled with disappointment.

"Hayden is here," he said after taking a bite of her burger. "If I stick around Chicago, it'll give him an excuse to run off again when the next woman comes along."

She gripped the arms of the plastic chair and watched in amazement as he polished off the rest of her cheeseburger, then attacked her uneaten French fries with gusto. He was completely oblivious to the fact he'd just crushed the slim hope she hadn't even realized she'd been harboring of something more lasting between them. Something worthy of that very special magic neither of them could deny existed without being dishonest to themselves and each other.

"I hate to be the one to point out the obvious, but he

did manage to get you home from the Navy. You don't have any guarantee that a little thing like geography is going to stop him from doing something like this again."

"You're right. I don't."

"New York is a long way from Illinois," she said around the sudden lump in her throat. She was being silly and she knew it, but she couldn't help herself. Sometime between this morning and this afternoon, she'd managed to convince herself there could be something more between them than fun and games. So much for Carly's Law, she thought. She'd not only broken every rule she could think of since running away, but she'd even gone so far as to bend her own laws.

"I know it is, Carly," he said quietly. He leveled his gaze on her, the intensity in his eyes shooting straight through to her heart. A heart she could swear was going to break. "After next week you'll be gone anyway, so why do you care where I end up?"

She looked away so he wouldn't see the pain she was certain shone in her own gaze. "I could stay."

"With no job?"

She looked back at him. How had it happened? How or why had she fallen for Cooper? It didn't make any sense. She'd wanted to spread her wings and taste life on her own terms, not fall for a bartender with his own life in turmoil. Then again, she thought, not much in her life made sense these days, and she felt as if she was simply drifting from day to day with little or no direction. So what if she'd been attempting to find a job? She hadn't found one and her prospects were dwindling. Without a real future, she couldn't stay in Chicago, and they both knew it.

"I could if I had a reason to stay," she said. "Can you give me a reason to stay in Chicago, Cooper?"

She held her breath. There. She'd said it. She'd boldly taken the risk. She might not have come right out and asked him if they had a future together, but while stubborn, Cooper Wilde was not stupid. The look of panic in his eyes told her loud and clear he knew exactly what she was asking.

"I'm sorry, Carly," he said after nearly a minute ticked by. "I can't do that."

She looked away so he wouldn't see the tears that blurred her vision. She'd taken the risk. And lost.

CARLY TRIED NOT to give Cooper's refusal to give her a reason to stay in Chicago any thought. Unfortunately, her mind had other plans, since that was all she thought about for the rest of the afternoon and well into the night.

By ten o'clock, she'd come to the conclusion that Cooper Wilde was a big fat chicken. He was afraid. Of what, she didn't know for certain, but she had a sneaking suspicion it had to do with this irresponsible uncle of his, and she was determined to find out if she was right. Of course, she had to speak to him in order to flesh out the truth, and they hadn't uttered a word to each other in over eight hours.

"Hey Carly," Joe Lanford called to her above Styx's "Renegade" playing on the jukebox. "How 'bout another round for me an' Benny?"

Carly pulled two beers from the cooler and set them on the round black tray. She carried them over to the pool table that Benny and Joe had been hanging around since they'd arrived over two hours ago. Tonight, the bar had a steady flow of customers, but it wasn't half as busy as she'd hoped. She wanted something to keep her mind off Cooper and his unwillingness to admit there was something happening between them. Unfortunately, she had more than enough down time to sit and moon over a man too stupid to see they were made for each other.

"What's got you looking so down in the dumps, Carly?" Benny asked, taking the beer from the tray. "I ain't seen you smile all night."

She handed Joe his beer and collected their empty bottles. "Nothing," she said, turning to clear away an empty table.

Joe followed her to the table. "Aw now, you can tell us if somethin's botherin' ya'. We're friends, remember?" Joe said, then flashed her a wide grin.

She supposed he did have a point. After all, she'd cried in front of them a week ago. But how did she begin to explain what she felt for Cooper? How could she tell them that though she'd been about to marry another man a week ago, what she felt for Cooper didn't even come close to rational, especially when she couldn't begin to understand her own feelings?

Her emotions, as well as her life, should have disaster zone stamped all over them. Again.

Benny joined Joe at the table she wiped down after removing the empty glassware. "You still worried 'bout that groom you dumped?" Benny asked, slipping his beefy arm around her shoulders in a gesture of comfort.

"You're gonna make her cry again," Joe scolded Benny.

She gave Joe a weak grin when Benny affectionately tightened his hold. "I'm not going to cry," she told them, even though that's exactly what she felt like doing.

Benny's puffy face spread into a wide grin, showing her his missing tooth. "Then what's the matter?" Benny asked. "You do look like you're gonna start wailin' again."

"Very funny, Benny," she said, aiming for lighthearted and coming in drastically short of her goal.

The hair on the back of Carly's neck tingled. She angled her head to look over Benny's beefy arm, not surprised to find Cooper standing a few inches away. The hard glint in his eyes, something she'd never seen before, did surprise her.

"I suggest you get your hands off my waitress and go back to shooting pool," Cooper practically growled from beside her.

Joe set his beer on the table. "Take it easy, Coop," he warned. "Ain't nothin' goin' on here."

Benny turned, his arm still around Carly, pulling her with him until they both faced a very angry Cooper. "What's your problem, Wilde?"

Cooper's arms were crossed and his feet were braced apart. He looked relaxed, except Carly knew better. He was coiled tight and ready for action, and she didn't have to be a Rhodes scholar to know why.

"You and your hands all over my waitress." Cooper's voice was filled with a deadly calm that made her nervous. She'd grown up in a house full of women. Out-of-control female hormones she understood. Unruly testosterone was definitely foreign territory.

"Cooper, he's not do—"

"Stay out of this, Carly," he shot at her, still keeping his threatening gaze locked on Benny.

"I will not," she shot back.

"Get your hands off her, West," he demanded in that same quiet voice, completely ignoring her. "Now."

"You better let her go, Benny," Joe told his friend.

She couldn't believe this was happening. For a guy who acted as if he couldn't care less whether or not she stayed in Chicago, he certainly was behaving like a jealous idiot. "Don't do this," she said to Benny, when his arm tightened around her shoulders.

"It's okay, Carly. I won't hurt him...too much," Benny said, gently pushing Carly behind him. "You wanna step outside, Wilde? Let's go."

Carly peered around Benny to look up at Cooper. "Don't you dare," she said, but he didn't even bother to glance in her direction.

"Okay boys," Karen called out, coming from behind the bar. "That's enough." She stepped between Cooper and Benny and looked from one to the other. "Or I'm gonna put you both in the corner until you can play nice together."

Neither man moved. "I said that's enough," Karen's voice was firm. "Coop, I need another keg of light beer. Would you mind getting it for me?"

Cooper stalked past Carly, but not before shooting her a glance that surprised the life right out of her. He blamed her. She saw it in those dark eyes. For reasons she didn't quite understand, he blamed her for the testosterone battle he'd been engaged in, as if it was her doing.

Well, she hadn't done anything wrong, and she refused to allow him to lay the blame at her feet. She'd had just about enough of Cooper and his damned seesawing back and forth. The man gave out more mixed signals than a faulty traffic light.

And as far as she was concerned, the collision that just took place was going to be the last.

11

Rule 11: A lady must always remember, a gentleman never buys the cake if he's given free samples to satisfy his hunger.

COOPER SAT ON the steps leading to the apartment and lowered his head. He'd stepped outside for some fresh air in a vain attempt to cool his temper. He couldn't explain what had come over him, other than a serious and unreasonable bout of jealousy he had no business feeling when he'd seen Benny holding Carly.

He'd not only acted like a first-class fool, and over a woman, no less, but he'd behaved no better than his uncle. He accepted full responsibility for his irrational behavior. What else could a guy with a defective gene pool do?

The back door to the bar squeaked, then slammed shut, followed by the crunch of gravel beneath feminine footsteps. He didn't need to look up to know Carly had followed him. His body automatically zeroed in on her.

"Something is seriously wrong with you."

"Go back inside, Carly," he warned. She was the last person he wanted to see right now.

"Forget it," she said, moving to sit beside him on the wooden steps. "I'm not going anywhere. At least not until you tell me what your problem is."

"Frustration," Cooper muttered, then shook his

head. "You better go back inside before you get into any more trouble."

"I wasn't in trouble in the first place," she complained, crossing her arms over her bare knees. She wore a pair of olive green shorts and a bright tropical-print tank top, leaving far too much of her lightly tanned skin exposed for his peace of mind. "Benny was just being nice."

"That's not what it looked like to me."

She let out a hefty sigh filled with the same frustration he'd been feeling since she'd barged into his life. "You're being completely unreasonable, not to mention illogical," she told him. "You tell me you can't give me any reason to stay in Chicago, yet you act like a major moron over something completely innocent. Benny wouldn't do anything to hurt me."

He glanced over at her, and the look in her eyes nearly had him coming off the steps and walking away. Determination, the same determination he had admired, he now despised. She was going to force him to face things he didn't want to face, like a past he'd spent his entire adult life running from. They really did have a lot in common, he thought bitterly. And running topped the list of comparisons.

"You don't know that," he said eventually.

"I only know what you've told me, Cooper," she stated reasonably. "What you've told me and what I saw for myself, which was you overreacting to a situation that didn't even exist in the first place."

He turned away, hating the accusation almost as much as he despised the truth of her astute summation. "I know," he admitted. "I'm sorry."

"I think you owe Benny the apology," she chastised in a gentle tone. "What's going on, Coop?"

I can't stop thinking about you.

He kept the thought, and the truth, to himself. Running and avoiding serious relationships had become such a habit for him, he didn't know how to take a step in any other direction. He wanted Carly. He wanted her so bad he ached. But fighting his attraction for her was quickly becoming a battle he was convinced he'd lose, and one that would confirm the truth. He was a Wilde, after all, and therefore doomed.

"I knew you were trouble the minute you walked into the bar," he told her, shifting his gaze to the cars parked across the quiet side street. "I just didn't realize exactly how much."

"Why do you keep saying that? I haven't done anything wrong."

He laughed, but it sounded hollow, even to him. He'd always prided himself on his intelligence, for being a whole lot smarter about the opposite sex than his mother and uncle. He'd managed thus far to convince himself he was superior, but he realized now he'd merely been taking the easy way out by steering clear of serious relationships. By doing so, he'd managed to avoid facing the truth—that he really was no different.

He shifted on the step to face her. "You don't have to *do* anything," he told her. "You're here, and for me, that's trouble enough. You're a distraction I didn't want. The Wildes have a long-standing reputation for making bad choices. My mother did, and my uncle still does. No matter how hard I try to deny it, I guess I do, too."

She had the audacity to grin. "I'm a bad choice?"

The need to touch her was strong, to reassure her in some way *she* wasn't bad, just a bad choice for him. He gave in to the need by lifting his hand and gently smoothing his knuckles down her satiny cheek. "You're real bad," he said gruffly. "I can't think of anything but you. I thought I had everything planned, but you're easily shooting it all to hell."

Her lashes fluttered closed and she turned her face toward his hand. "Your plans don't have to change," she stated reasonably. Too bad reasonable and Carly just didn't add up to him not losing himself.

He lowered his hand, settling it over her knee. "Do you really think I'd want to move to New York if you're staying in Chicago?"

"But you said—"

"I know what I said," he interrupted. "I lied, okay? I can give you a hundred reasons to stay in Chicago, but it'd never work."

She picked up his hand and laced their fingers together. "How do you know that unless you're willing to give it a try?" she asked, avoiding his eyes by studying their joined hands.

"We come from different backgrounds. You're small-town, with roots that probably date back to the first pioneers in Illinois. I've made it a habit to be on the move so long that I don't think I know how to stay in one place."

"You've never tried," she countered, still not looking at him. "The navy sent you—"

With his free hand, he lifted her chin. The tenderness and uncertainty in her turquoise eyes tore at his heart, a place far too rusty and unused. "I have nothing to offer you, Princess. I'm almost broke. The bar, which still belongs to Hayden, is nearly bankrupt. I'm close to thirty years old and I'm technically still living at home. How pathetic is that?"

"Those things don't matter to me."

"They do to me," he argued. "You deserve better."

"Next Thursday night you'll have a good start at making back the money you've put into the bar. The rest isn't important."

He dropped his hand and stood, shoving his fists into the front pockets of his trousers. "You still don't get it, do you?" he said, frustrated by her unwillingness to agree with his assessment of their situation. "You're all I think about. You've managed to distract me to the point that I really don't give a rip about anything but you."

She crossed her arms over her knees again and looked up at him with that damned determined glint in her eyes. "That is so untrue. You're worried about your future. Doesn't that tell you something?"

"It's not what's important to me," he shot at her in frustration. "Not right here. Not right now."

Carly figured she had two choices as Cooper brushed past her and climbed the stairs to the apartment without so much as another glance in her direction. She could either follow him, or she could leave him alone and go back to the bar to help Karen.

Based on the things he'd said, she knew he was feeling vulnerable. Cooper wasn't the type of guy who was comfortable talking about his feelings. She realized he'd avoided developing relationships for so long that he didn't have any idea how to do anything else. He was pushing her away, not because he really thought she deserved better, but because he was afraid. Afraid he'd follow in the footsteps of the rest of his family. If she truly wanted something more between them, then it was going to be up to her to show him they could have a relationship without him losing his identity in the process.

Wasn't that what it really was all about? It was why she'd run away to Chicago in the first place, because she also feared losing herself in a life that didn't truly belong to her, but to some archaic, idealistic viewpoint found only in the black-and-white reruns on *Nick at Nite.*

Cooper was doing the same thing, but for different reasons. He was running away from her now because he harbored a similar fear. Why hadn't she seen this sooner? As a kid, he'd had little control over his life, but instead was left to the chaotic whims of his caretakers. It made sense that he feared losing his identity if he allowed himself to follow his heart.

She'd wanted to taste life on her own terms, stop being the good girl and do things her way. She had wanted to control her own destiny, something she couldn't do stifled by the idealism of others. What Cooper wanted wasn't so different. She understood that now. He, too, wanted to maintain control, and by giving in to the unexplainable emotions between them, he held the misguided belief he'd relinquish what control he'd managed to acquire in recent years.

Now all she had to do was find a way to show him he couldn't be more wrong.

She climbed the stairs to the darkened apartment. A thin veil of moonlight slashed across the hardwood floor and illuminated the shadows of the living room. She peered into the darkness and found Cooper silhouetted against the twin windows overlooking the street below. He stood with his back to her, his hands stuffed into the front pockets of his khaki trousers, his head bent forward.

"Go back to the bar, Carly," he said, not bothering to

look in her direction. "Better yet, go back to wherever it is you've come from, before we're both sorry."

She ignored his warning and continued to cross the room toward him. He visibly stiffened.

"I come from Homer," she said. If she wanted him to trust her, then she couldn't very well continue avoiding the truth about herself. "It's a little town a couple of hours away. I've lived there all my life, except the four years I spent at the University of Indiana. Far enough away that I felt somewhat independent, but close enough that it was easy to come home for holidays and breaks, or for my sisters to visit on the occasional weekend."

He remained silent and kept his back toward her. Slowly, she eased around him until she was looking up at him. His eyes were hard, his body language equally hard and unyielding. She understood his battle now. She knew what it was like to lose herself in the dictates of others, to perform based on their actions and expectations. The circumstances may have been different for Cooper, but in the end, the results were all the same.

"You're right," she told him. "There are a lot of people who care about me and are probably worried about me, but I did get in touch with them to let them know I'm okay. I'm the youngest of seven daughters in a family that I never doubted loved me. There was nothing unstable about my home life. It was so disgustingly normal, I'd never have a thing to tell a shrink. Probably the only thing I can even say about my family is that they all have high expectations, for themselves and each other. Maybe you're right. I should go home, but I can't. Not yet. If I do, I'll be giving up what little I've managed to gain."

"I know all about gains, Princess." The bitterness in

his voice ripped through her chest like an arrow straight to her heart. He was hurt and afraid. She wanted to help ease his pain and set aside his fears. "When you walked into The Wilde Side, you threw mine back about ten years."

"That's not true," she said, shaking her head. "Neither one of us can lose anything by giving in to our attraction to each other. The only way you'll lose anything, Cooper, is if you let your fear keep you from what you really want."

He looked away, but not before she caught a hint of doubt in his eyes. Not doubt in what she was saying, but in what he believed.

"I want you, Cooper," she said quietly. "Can't we just capture this moment and figure the rest out later?"

He looked down at her, the internal struggle evident in his handsome face, in those dark, intense eyes. "You don't know what you're asking."

A tiny grin tugged her lips. She knew exactly what she was asking.

Carly's Law: Never buy a pair of shoes without trying them on first.

"Yes, Cooper," she said, sifting her fingers through his thick sable hair. "I know exactly what I'm asking. I'm asking you to make love to me. Make love to me and let me show you that you won't be losing anything."

She felt his hesitancy when his hands eased around her waist. Saw the fear and reluctance in his eyes slip away when he pulled her even closer. "Now there's where you're wrong, Princess."

She didn't have time to summon a reply because his mouth claimed hers in a hot, tongue-tangling kiss that had her toes curling and her insides melting. She moaned and twined her arms around his neck, pressing closer until the tips of her breasts rubbed against his chest. Curiosity and tension twisted inside her. Fate had brought them together, and tonight Carly planned to break the most important rule of all. She planned to give not only of her body, but of her heart, as well. Tonight they wouldn't deny their need and desire. She refused to accept anything less.

His hands slid from her waist to grip her hips, and he pulled her hard against him. A bolt of electricity shot through her at the intimate contact, pooling in her belly and lower, making her wet with fierce, insistent need. It was just a kiss and already she was burning up with desire.

He ran his hands up her sides to her arms, and she moved against him. He broke the kiss and pulled her arms from around his neck. Cool air washed over her, breaking the spell and bringing her erotic thoughts to a screeching halt.

"Princess, you're killing me." His voice was tight, his expression tighter. He didn't look angry or afraid. He looked...frustrated.

Feminine satisfaction made her smile, and she gave a throaty laugh she hardly recognized as her own. "The feeling is mutual, Wilde. And I suggest we stop this crazy denial and embark on something a little more satisfying."

She turned away and walked out of the living room and straight into his bedroom. She stopped at the doorway and looked over her shoulder at him. "Coming?" she asked in the sultriest, sexiest voice she'd ever used.

The look in his eyes said he'd follow her just about anywhere at this point. She waited while he locked the front door before walking into the bedroom. As she closed the door behind them, he grabbed her wrist and pulled her against him. His arms slipped around her, and he held her tight. He was hard, he was all male. He was Cooper, the man who set her soul on fire and somehow had captured her heart.

She didn't need wine and candlelight. She needed him, and she planned to show him exactly how much.

"This won't change anything," he warned in a low voice before dipping his head lower.

"Yes, it will," she argued softly as his lips skimmed her throat. He nipped with his teeth, then soothed with his tongue until he reached her lips. A shiver passed through her and she moaned as his tongue slipped between her parted lips. Wrapping her arms around his neck, she slid her fingers into his hair and returned his kiss with a passion that would have surprised her if it'd been anyone else but Cooper. He brought out her passionate nature as no other man ever had, and she doubted ever would again.

Need twisted and knotted inside her, and when his hand slid along her hip and upward, to cup her breast, she moaned and arched against his palm. She wanted more. She wanted to feel his skin pressed against hers, to feel his body poised over hers, to feel him deep inside. She wanted him so much she ached, and he was her only remedy.

His mouth left hers and she whimpered in protest. Already her breath came in short gasps, her body burned with awakened passion. "To hell with rules," she whispered and strained toward him.

He chuckled and gave her a quick, hard kiss before setting her away from him. She stared at him, her mind and body screaming for him to come back and finish what he'd started. She hadn't played coy since she'd met him, and she wasn't about to start now.

Still facing him, she moved backward toward the bed and kicked off her sneakers, then reached for the snap of her shorts.

He moved in front of her and settled his hand over hers. "Don't," he said. "Let me."

"You want to undress me?"

His intense gaze darkened. "For starters," he said, flicking the snap with his fingers.

Her pulse quickened.

"And then..." he said, easing the shorts over her hips. The tip of his finger teased the top edge of her satin panties.

Her shorts hit the floor, along with her stomach.

"Then I'm going to make love to you, Carly. All. Night. Long."

Her breath rushed out of her. She had a feeling she was going to be receiving more than she'd bargained for—a whole lot more.

He traced a lazy pattern with his fingers just below the satin edge. Heat flowed through her and pooled in her tummy. Desire licked through her, and he was barely touching her.

Cooper shifted to ease the painful erection throbbing against the confines of his trousers and urged her down on the bed. Still fully clothed, he settled his body alongside hers, skimming his hand over her hip, then along the edge of the hot pink satin hiding her feminine secrets.

She tugged the tank top over her head and tossed it on the floor next to her shorts and sneakers. Her satin bra followed, freeing her full, round breasts. His hand caressed her hip, moved along her flat stomach and upward to cup her breast, his thumb teasing her nipple into a taut peak.

"You're so beautiful," he said, surprised by the gruff sound of his voice. He could lie like this and look at her all night. Touch her all night. Make her his in the most elemental way possible.

The turquoise in her eyes deepened. "I want..." she said in a throaty whisper.

He dipped his head and tasted her skin. He breathed in her scent, something more intoxicating than any perfume company could ever hope to duplicate.

"What do you want, Princess?" he murmured. She trembled, effectively heightening his awareness to the point of pain. He knew she wasn't a virgin, but he'd bet she didn't have vast experience, either. He wanted to take things slow. To savor the moment for as long as possible, to build her awareness of him until they were both so mindless with need the only thing that mattered was pleasure. Pleasure he wanted—complete loss of control, he wouldn't allow.

She looked at him. There was no uncertainty in her eyes, but he detected a vulnerability that made him feel protective. "You," she said in a husky whisper. She looped her hand around his neck, drawing him closer. "I want you, Cooper. All of you."

Instead of pressing his lips to hers, he trailed a path from her throat down to the slope of her breasts. "I want to taste you," he whispered. She shivered when he laved her breast, then closed her eyes and moaned, a sexy little sound in the back of her throat that had his blood pumping fast.

Slow was going to kill him. He'd known she was trouble. He'd known it the moment she'd walked into his life, and he finally understood why—she made him want things he had no business wanting for himself. But that didn't stop him from skimming his hand up her legs to pull the last scrap of satin from her body.

She moaned when his hand brushed against her moist curls, a deep, throaty purr that nearly brought him out of his skin. His mouth left her breast and skimmed along her tummy. He rubbed his thumb over her feminine folds and she arched against his hand, nearly snapping the tenuous thread he fought to keep his control intact. "I love how you respond to me."

Carly shifted her hips restlessly, knowing Cooper wouldn't stop until she fell apart in his arms. As a lover, he was completely unselfish, except he kept the one thing from her she wanted the most: she wanted him as mindless as he made her feel. "I have to touch you," she said, before another soft moan escaped her lips. "I want you to feel the way I'm feeling."

Before he drove her completely out of her mind and sent her over the edge into sweet oblivion, she reached for his belt and fumbled with the catch. "Get naked, Cooper. Now."

He chuckled, and continued to draw more lazy circles against her skin with his tongue. "We've got all night."

She sucked in a sharp breath when his finger slipped deep inside her. She stopped fumbling with the catch of his belt and gripped the patterned quilt in her hands, having no other option than to give in to the storm of intensity and allow Cooper to lead her to that place where rational thought failed to exist and only sensation remained.

Ripples of heat purled across her skin as his mouth dipped lower, his breath warm against her center, his tongue hot and cool at the same time as he teased past her feminine folds. His lips closed over her and he gently suckled while his fingers continued their intimate exploration until her body arched toward the wild sensations raging through her.

"Cooper," she cried out when the tension built fast and she came in a rush so powerful her body quaked with tiny tremors. He gently eased her back down to earth, his mouth moving along her body to capture her lips in a kiss so hot and erotic she thought for certain she'd come again.

Somehow, he managed to deepen the kiss even more, the movements of his tongue and mouth in perfect rhythm with the movements of his hands. She craved his body, she wanted to feel him inside her, wanted his body to mate with hers. She wanted him to lose control and make her completely his.

She slipped her hands into his hair and pulled him away. "This isn't going to work," she said.

"I think it's working great," he said. He attempted to lower his head, but she held him away.

"Not like this," she said. Not unless he was willing to take the complete journey with her.

He slowly moved his hand away. "What are you talking about?"

"Not like this," she said again. "I want to make love to you, Cooper. But if you can't be here with me, then forget it."

12

Rule 12: Under no circumstances should a lady ever discuss S. E. X.

"EXACTLY WHERE the hell do you think I am?"

Carly swung her legs to the floor and sat on the edge of the bed. Ignoring his angry retort, she reached for her tank top and slipped it over her head. "You're not here with me, that's for sure." Confronting Cooper about something this important didn't bother her. Doing it in the buff was another matter altogether. Her confidence only stretched so far.

"Carly—"

"No, Coop," she snatched her panties from the floor and stepped into them before turning back to face him. "I want this. I've never wanted anything more, but we *both* have to be here to enjoy it."

He tossed the pillows behind him and leaned against the plain pine headboard. His glare was angry and a dangerous light flashed in his eyes. "I don't know what you're talking about. I'm here, dammit."

She moved back to the bed and sat facing him, more concerned with reaching him emotionally than his grousing and complaining. Frustration was something she understood, especially when dealing with Cooper Wilde. "Maybe physically," she explained, "but not emotionally."

He let out a rough sigh filled with equal amounts of frustration and irritation. "What do you want from me?" he demanded, shoving his hands through his hair.

She probably wanted too much, but could settle for nothing less than *all* of him. Too many years of habitually withholding emotion could very well make it impossible for him to give her what she needed. She needed him with her, in every sense of the word. They had the physical part down to a science. He could make her body hum with anticipation and sing with pleasure. But all those times she'd eavesdropped on her sisters' discussions around the big table in the kitchen of the parsonage, were about to pay off in spades. She'd heard enough of their hushed conversations to know that there was more to making love than the physical act. Without emotion, it was just sex.

She wanted more than sex, and emotionally, Cooper was miles away.

"You're holding back." She moved closer and settled her hand on his thigh. "I want to make love to you, Cooper. To *all* of you."

Panic filled his eyes. "It's not that simple."

Slowly, she ran her hand over the soft fabric of his trousers. "It *is* that simple," she told him in a husky whisper. She knew he was afraid, and she thought she understood his fear. But it was just the two of them now, and throwing his life into turmoil wasn't her goal. She wanted him. It really *was* that simple.

"Cooper, you excite me beyond belief. You make me feel the way no man has ever made me feel before. But I want you here with me. Otherwise it's just sex."

Her fingers inched up his thigh. His hand clamped down on hers and held it tight. "You don't know what you're asking," he said, his voice tight with the emotions he was afraid to unleash.

"Yes," she said quietly, pulling her hand from beneath his to continue up his thigh. "I do."

He stared at her, a series of emotions flickering across his handsome face. Panic, and something else she couldn't define but suspected could be caring, which no doubt would spook a guy like Cooper. She shifted even closer to him, and then rose to her knees.

"You asked me what I wanted from you." Bracketing his hips with her knees, she sat on his lap. "I said I wanted you."

He shot her a look filled with heat, but not the kind she hoped to see. She was pushing him, but it was the only way she knew to get what she wanted from him.

"I'm here, dammit!" he thundered.

She shook her head and planted her hands on his hard chest. "I want more than just your body, Cooper." She smoothed her hands down his lean torso before tugging the black polo shirt from his pants.

Her hands slipped beneath the shirt and pressed against the warmth of his skin.

"What else is there?" he asked.

She lifted his shirt and leaned forward to press her lips against his chest. "Your soul," she said, then tasted his heated flesh. The muscles flexed and moved as she wound her way down his body, her tongue circling his belly button, while her fingers worked at unfastening his trousers.

He sucked in a sharp breath when she eased his zipper down. She lifted her head and looked into his dark, intense eyes. "I want your soul, Cooper Wilde," she whispered.

A low growl tore from his chest. He yanked his shirt

off, then hers before he rolled her beneath him in one brisk move that nearly took her breath away. He shoved his hands into her curls, holding her head between his hands. "You'll be getting a hell of a lot more than you ever bargained for, Princess," he said roughly, then slanted his mouth over hers in a kiss ten times more possessive than any other...until now.

Now he took. Now he demanded everything she had to give and more. It was no less than she expected from him, no less than what she needed from him, and she surrendered to the blissful promise of the heat and passion Cooper had so foolishly attempted to withhold from her.

His hands roamed her body, hot and insistent against her skin, effortlessly removing the flimsy panties she'd wasted her time slipping back on. She in turn explored every inch of his big, muscular body, urging him out of his trousers and briefs until they were skin to skin, man to woman.

She pushed at his shoulders, then moved on top of him, winding her body along the long, firm length of his with her mouth and hands. She eased her fingers around his erection, then circled the tip with her tongue. A rough breath eased out between his teeth, then he groaned, the sound low and primal, coming up from somewhere deep within his chest. When she slipped her mouth over him, his hips bucked and he gripped her shoulders. He tried to pull her back up his body, but she ignored his demands and concentrated on loving him with her mouth until she sensed him close to the brink.

She kissed her way back up his torso, stopping to tease his flat nipples with her tongue. His hands slid into her hair and he guided her mouth to his for a hot, deep kiss. Easing onto her knees, she straddled his hips and rocked against the hard length of his erection. Tiny sparks ignited with each move, slowly fanning the flames simmering just below the surface of his control.

With their mouths still joined, he gripped her hips and guided her over him, and then he thrust upward, making her completely his—heart, body and soul.

Cooper was lost. The control he'd worked so hard to maintain had slipped and was close to disappearing completely. There would be no turning back now. Carly was his.

Making love to her had to be the most idiotic stunt of his life, but only a natural disaster could stop him from the path he'd chosen to follow tonight. They may have only known each other for a short time, but in that time, they'd become friends, business partners in a strange, misguided sense, and now as he'd predicted, lovers.

He ended the kiss and watched as her lashes fluttered. He looked into her bright turquoise eyes. Even though the emotion in her gaze spooked him, no woman had ever looked at him the way Carly was now, with caring that gripped his heart and need that fueled his passion.

"Cooper," she whispered, his name a husky purr of sound that nearly had him coming. He balled his hands into fists, fighting to hold on to the last thin thread of control.

"All of you," she whispered huskily.

He wanted to take things slow, but need pulsed through him in hot waves. She refused slow. She demanded more. She demanded everything.

He gave up the fight, unleashing what was left of his control. Intense pleasure ripped through him when she pressed down against him and leaned back, her fingers lightly brushing the inside of his thighs. He moaned and thrust higher, his world narrowing to just the two of them and the reckless need that wouldn't allow either of them to stop.

Heaven help him, stopping was the last thing on his mind.

She tossed her head back and rode him with a passion that matched his own, now that she'd forced him to unleash all of it on her. "Come for me, Carly," he rasped, driving them both higher and higher. "Come for me again."

He reached between them, sliding his fingers over her slick folds, pressing his thumb against her most sensitive place until she arched and peaked, his name falling from her lips in a lusty cry.

Before her tremors ceased, he rolled her to her back and continued to thrust into her. She wrapped her legs around his waist, their bodies parting and meeting on their own sensual level, their hearts meeting and their souls melding until the tension coiled so tightly inside him burst free from the chains of control he'd unwisely believed he could maintain.

He felt her reaching the edge again, reaching for it desperately, straining for the pleasure that belonged to both of them. Her body trembled and he carried her closer until she was shuddering around him, milking him with her body as another earth-shattering orgasm racked her. She pushed him into the maelstrom of emotion and need, until he finally, blessedly, found his own release, one so forceful it crashed through his body in hard, pounding waves.

He felt her move, felt her hands trace lazy patterns over his sweat-slicked back, felt her lips press against his shoulder and over his chest. No woman had ever urged him to lose control, or gave and took with such honesty as Carly. He never imagined anything like what he'd just experienced.

Driven to the brink by a curvy bombshell who tested his patience and thought his control a waste of her time, he'd given in to elemental desire and the deep primal need to make her completely his. She overwhelmed him. She demanded nothing less than everything he had to give. A demand she'd practically forced him to meet that had left them both sated and exhausted.

With Carly, there was no maintaining control, there was only passion and heat. There were too many emotions to name, but one that stood above the rest. One he feared most of all.

The one that had him giving Carly his soul.

COOPER HELD Carly in his arms while she slept spread half over his body and half on the mattress. A grin tugged his lips. His princess was pooped!

As absolutely wonderful as their lovemaking had been, he cursed himself. Not because he'd submitted to Carly's demands and had given himself to her wholly, but because of something much more important than his own fears. He'd behaved irresponsibly, and that was unforgivable.

She stirred, her delicate hand flexing against his chest. Seconds later, he felt her tongue tease his nipple. He hardened in a flash.

Resisting the incredible urge to pull her beneath him again, he slipped his hand under her chin to tip her head back so she was looking at him. She looked sleepy and satisfied, and despite the seriousness of the situation caused by his complete loss of control, he couldn't help the surge of male pride gripping him. "I'm sorry, Princess."

She gave him one of those sleepy, spunky grins that fired his blood. "You're supposed to be thanking me, Wilde, not apologizing," she quipped, then slid her hand down his stomach and beneath the sheet draped over his hips.

He shook his head and stopped her before she reached her intended destination. "We didn't use protection."

She cleared her throat and pulled her hand from his, easing onto her side of the bed. "I know," she said quietly, tucking the sheet under her chin.

He flipped on the bedside lamp, then turned to his side. Using his elbow for support, he propped his head in his hand before brushing a springy platinum curl from her face and tucking it behind her ear. "Carly—"

She reached for his hand and held it next to her cheek. Closing her eyes, she brushed her face back and forth along the back of his hand. "Let's not worry about it now, okay?"

They were both pros when it came to running. Well, this time neither one of them had the luxury of running away from the subject, no matter how much she might want to avoid discussing it.

"We need to talk about this," he said.

She dropped his hand and looked at him, her gaze ruthlessly direct. "We had unprotected sex," she said. "I know the risks we just took, Cooper, and I take part of that responsibility, too."

"Not only is what we just did suicidal in this day and age," he told her, "but you do know where babies come from, don't you?"

She sighed and turned onto her back to look up at the ceiling. "Yes, Cooper," she said, a note of sarcasm lacing her sweet voice. "I think I have a pretty good ideas where babies come from, and I doubt it's from French-kissing like my older sister, Jilly, tried to tell me when I was nine years old."

A smile lurked around his mouth. Imagining Carly as a curious child wasn't tough. Imagining her swollen with his child nearly took his breath away and didn't fill him with as much dread as he might have imagined. Roots had never been all that important to him, at least not as important as keeping at bay the disastrous emotions that had his uncle shirking his responsibilities or his mother chasing one guy after the next, looking for something that didn't exist. But suddenly, the idea of settling down—in particular, settling down with Carly—held a whole lot of appeal. Too bad he had nothing substantial to offer her.

She turned her head on the pillow to look at him again. "Do we really have to be so serious right now? I can think of lots of other things we could be doing."

He grinned. So could he. None of which required much discussion. "We could very well end up being serious for about eighteen years or longer."

She plucked at the sheet and looked up at him curiously. "This is about more than just a possible unplanned pregnancy, isn't it?"

Unable to resist touching her, he spanned the small space separating them and pulled her closer. "I know you're not experienced," he said, trailing the tips of his fingers over her shoulder until she trembled lightly in his arms, "but I want you to know that I'm healthy."

Carly stared into Cooper's dark eyes, the intensity holding her spellbound in the dim golden light. "In case it slipped your attention, while I might be low mileage, I have been test-driven before."

He didn't smile, or respond to her quip. He was intent on having a serious conversation. She sighed. "I know what you're trying to ask. I've only made love to one other person, and it was protected."

"Your fiancé?"

She nodded. She didn't bother to tell him she could probably count the times she and Dean had made love on one hand, using only two fingers! In most things, she was pretty much an overachiever. Sex wasn't one of them. Sex with Cooper could definitely change her status.

"And that's it?" he asked incredulously.

She rolled her eyes in exasperation. Her inexperience wasn't something she was exactly proud of. "Yeah, so?"

He smiled at her, one of those lazy, comfortable ones that held absolutely no apology for his blatant prying into her pitiful sex life. "And what are you grinning for?" she asked, playfully poking one of his iron-hard biceps with the tip of her index finger.

Gentle laughter rumbled up from his chest, and he dipped his head and planted a quick, hard kiss on her lips, no less possessive than his usual toe-curlers.

She slipped her hand behind his neck and pulled him toward her. He leaned over her, using his arms to brace himself. "Feeling a little arrogant, aren't we?" she teased.

The laughter in his eyes faded, replaced by a gentle, tender light as he looked down at her. "You will tell me if you're pregnant, right?" His voice held an odd tightness in spite of his casual tone.

"If this is going to be a debate about a woman's right to choose—"

"I have a right to know," he interrupted harshly, a deep frown quickly falling in place.

Something was going on, and she wished he'd let her in on whatever it was. "*If* it happens, of course I'll tell you."

He visibly relaxed, heightening her curiosity. "Thank you."

"You surprise me, Coop. Most guys would be *worried* about a girl telling them that she's pregnant."

He shrugged. "I'm not most guys."

"Hmm," she murmured wickedly. She ran her hands over his wide shoulders and down his thick arms. "So I'm learning."

He didn't respond to her teasing. His expression was serious as he continued to look down at her. "My mother never told my father she was pregnant. I know what it's like to grow up without a father."

"I thought...I don't know what I thought," she said. "I guess I just assumed..."

"Wilde was my mother's maiden name," he told her. "Hayden is her brother."

"I didn't know."

"Does it matter?"

"Don't be ridiculous," she said quickly. "Of course it doesn't matter." They were hardly living in the dark ages, where things like parentage mattered. She'd fallen in love with Cooper for who he was, not whether his parents had been married at the time of his birth.

Now how on earth had that happened? she wondered. Easy, she thought. Cooper made her feel all those things her sisters had always talked about. The kind of things Chickie and Alison had said you felt when you were truly in love.

Cooper was kind and he cared about people. He worried about his uncle and what would happen to him if The Wilde Side went under, so much so that he'd put his own money into a failing business. Considering the financial state of the bar, she knew he really couldn't afford to keep Karen on the payroll, but she had a daughter to support, and he wasn't going to let anything happen to them, either.

When she'd passed out in the ladies' room, he hadn't called the police, but had carried her upstairs to his apartment and even let her live with him and invade his ordered life. He didn't complain when she left the newspaper cluttering up the table every morning, or say a word about all those satin and lacy under things she hung in the bathroom to dry, though she knew it had to make a neat fanatic like him absolutely crazy. He'd even bought her tea because he knew she preferred it over coffee in the morning. Who wouldn't fall in love with a man like that, especially one who excited her beyond belief?

But where did that leave them? Had things changed all that much just because they'd made love? If she'd learned anything about Cooper this past week, it was that he had an incredible stubborn streak, even stronger than her own. He also harbored antiquated ideas about a man's role and had made a point of telling her he had nothing to offer her.

Materialism meant nothing. All she wanted was his heart, something she wasn't sure he'd be quite as willing to give.

She looped her arms around his neck and looked into those dark eyes that seemed to see straight to her soul, right into that place where she harbored hope for the future. A future for them.

"Where you come from isn't what's important," she told him. "It's who you are that matters."

Relief crossed his face seconds before he lowered his head and did a stellar job of curling her toes.

13

Rule 13: A lady may be a patron of the arts, but she should never be a participant.

COOPER REMOVED the note Carly had taped to the coffeemaker that said she was downstairs getting ready for ladies' night. Since he'd bought the paint she'd wanted yesterday afternoon, he figured she'd decided to get started on the bar's face-lift. He planned to join her soon. Right now, he had some hard choices to make. Choices that not only would affect him, but also Hayden.

He couldn't afford to keep The Wilde Side open much longer, not without completely draining his bank account. He had doubts that ladies' night would be the success Carly was hoping for, which meant he needed an alternate plan.

The time had come to face reality, and only one option made sense. Soon The Wilde Side would be no more.

He poured himself a second cup of coffee and carried it back to the dining table. Hercules lumbered behind him and plopped down at his feet, purring and pawing at the laces of his tennis shoes.

He looked down at the cat who'd been his only company until Carly had so effortlessly disrupted his life. "So what does an ex-navy SEAL do for the rest of his life?" he asked, reaching down to scratch the big cat's tummy. Herc blinked his green eyes at him, then went back to batting the laces of Coop's shoes. "Yeah, thanks for the great advice, buddy."

His training was in security systems. To start his own company would take a heck of a lot more money than what he had left. He didn't like the idea of having to settle for working for someone else, but until he could recoup the money he'd lost on the bar, his choices were limited. Selling the building would repay him, but that could take months. Until his missing-in-action uncle decided to return, he couldn't even put the property on the market, since Hayden was still the legal owner.

The thought of closing down the bar didn't fill him with as much dread or guilt as he'd imagined. The neighborhood tavern was part of a bygone era. Times changed and life went on, leaving behind memories, some good, some bad. Much of his life had revolved around The Wilde Side in one way or another. Despite his mother and uncle's obsession with the opposite sex and how it had affected him growing up, he had to admit that many of his memories were of the happier moments and the way his family used to involve the neighborhood in various functions. As Marty had said, times had been different then, and any attempt to resurrect that kind of activity would no doubt close the bar down a heck of a lot faster than any rapidly depleting bank account.

He glanced out the window overlooking the side street below. Quite a few cars were parked along the curb, unusual for a Saturday morning considering the bar wasn't open for business for another couple of hours. He shrugged and sipped his coffee. Probably one of the other businesses on the block having a sale of some sort.

Monday morning he'd start the job search. His ten years in the navy had garnered a few contacts, and the time had come for a little networking. Once he had a solid line on a job, he'd make the announcement about closing the bar, and then he'd be free to concentrate on his relationship with Carly.

He shook his head and stood. The last thing he'd ever expected to be doing was seriously concentrating on a woman. He wasn't exactly making plans to permanently include her in his life, but even that option failed to cause the hair on the back of his neck to rise or his chest to tighten with panic. Maybe it was because Carly wasn't just any woman, he reminded himself as he rinsed his mug and set it in the dishwasher. She was the woman who'd demanded nothing less than his soul.

He didn't know what the future held for them, or if they even had a future together. One thing he did know for certain: he didn't like the thought of her going back to Homer to settle into small-town life, taking a job she didn't want or living her life according to the dictates of her family. Maybe because the Carly he knew was so far removed from the young woman she had claimed to once be, or maybe because of something deeper and more emotional that he refused to acknowledge. He didn't exactly see forever in the forecast, but so long as he maintained his focus on his own goals and responsibilities, he couldn't deny the possibilities of a relationship.

And the possibilities were endless.

CARLY STOPPED the tape player, struggling to maintain her patience. The "doll-babies," as Karen had dubbed

them, weren't professionals, a fact she'd been reminding herself of constantly all morning. They were just
some nice guys out to make a few extra bucks for whatever reason.

"Okay fellas," she said when she turned back to face
them. "Listen up. I want you to do it like this."

For the fourth time, she showed them what she
deemed the proper way to move their hips in time to
the music. For the most part, they were pretty good.
Amateurs, but still good enough to cause more than a
few women to reach into their wallets and buy more
drinks than they should, and offer tips to keep them
shimmying their collective backsides to the beat of the
music. Money is what it's all about, she thought. Something she hoped they made a ton of so Cooper
wouldn't bust a gasket when he found out exactly
what she was up to.

Vinny, the friend Ken had said he'd bring along,
shook his head in dismay. "Carly, there's no way I can
move like that," he said, pointing at her as she swayed
her hips back and forth. "I'm a med student, not an exotic dancer."

She glanced over her shoulder at him and smiled.
"Just think of it as operating to music. And you're getting paid to do it, too."

"I don't think those are exactly the kind of moves I'll
be making in the operating room," Vinny countered,
his dark brown eyes filling with humor.

"You will if you find yourself a sexy young nurse,"
Ken teased his friend, causing the rest of the group to
chuckle.

"Okay now. Move with me," Carly said to them.
"One, two, three..."

She stifled a grin at Vinny's attempt. "Keep moving," she told the others, then crossed the area she'd commandeered as a dance floor to stand in front of Vinny. "Like this," she instructed, hiding a grin. Hooking her fingers in the belt loops at his side, she urged him to wiggle and shimmy as she'd shown him.

"That's good," she encouraged when his movements stopped being so mechanical and were a little more fluid. "Keep it going, fellas."

She turned away to start the tape player again. "One more time from the top. And don't worry, you *will* be ready by Thursday." They had to be, or she'd lose more money than she could afford, and her goal to help Cooper earn back some of what he'd lost would be a total flop.

"Good!" she called out as her boys shimmied, shook and ground their hips to the beat of the music. Pleased with their progress, she walked back to the front to show them another move they could incorporate into their own routines. "Watch me," she said over her shoulder, then froze.

Cooper loomed in the doorway, a solid wall of very irritated male. Her heart stuttered behind her ribs. Karen had warned her he'd be furious when he found out exactly what kind of fund-raising activities she had planned. Furious didn't begin to explain the horrified and livid expression thinning his lips and filling his eyes with a different kind of heat.

One by one, the guys stopped their dancing to determine why their instructor was biting her lip, and why her eyes were darting nervously around the room. She looked like a frightened bunny about to bolt from a hungry wolf.

She wasn't *really* looking for a place to hide. Well, maybe for a while. Just until Cooper cooled down.

She sucked in a deep breath and crossed to the bar to turn off the tape player. Play it cool, she thought. Pretend he doesn't look ready to blow.

"Cooper." She cleared her throat. "I'd like you to meet your new employees."

He stepped into the main area of the bar and glared angrily down at her. "Why would my 'new employees' be dancing?" he asked, his voice as tight as his jawline.

"Well," she started with a voice as tremulous as the grin she attempted, "they're rehearsing for ladies' night."

A muscle twitched in his cheek. Probably from grinding his teeth. She turned back to face the guys but could still feel Cooper's laser-hot glare piercing her. "Go ahead and take five, guys."

"Take the rest of the day," Cooper barked, looking ferocious. He snagged her wrist and headed toward the office.

"Ten," she called out to them before she disappeared down the hallway. "We still have work to do."

"Like hell you do," Cooper growled, shoving open the door to the small, cramped office. "This ends now, Carly."

She sighed when he slammed the door shut behind them. "You know, you really shouldn't be so rude to them," she said, tugging her hand from his grasp. "Not when they're the reason The Wilde Side is going to start seeing a profit."

"Profit my..." He let out a harsh breath and shoved a hand through his hair. "You're not doing this, Carly."

She bristled at his high-handed attitude, but tamped down her irritation at another one of his prehistoric displays. What she was doing was too important to get lost in a battle of wills, even if this was one battle she was determined to emerge as the victor.

"You need to make money or close the bar," she stated in a much more reasonable tone than he was intent on using. "That's what I'm doing, Coop. I've found something that'll make money like you wouldn't believe."

He propped his backside against the edge of the desk and folded his arms over his chest. "And this is what your *research* told you?"

She ignored his sarcasm and his rising tone of voice, which she'd heard just about enough of recently. Cooper might be stubborn, but he wasn't completely unreasonable. If he was willing to listen to her, she could make him see her plan was practically a guaranteed success. "The cash registers never stopped ringing up sales at the places Karen and I went to. You should have seen it. The amount of money these nightclubs make is incredible."

"Exactly where did you and Karen go?" he asked in a quiet voice that held enough of a threat to warn her of a pending explosion.

She put some distance between them by circling the desk and dropping into the leather chair. "Just a few nightclubs that featured male exotic dancers," she answered in a rush.

She bit her lip and waited for him to erupt like an angry volcano. Considering his reaction last night when Benny merely put his arm around her to comfort her, she wasn't quite sure what to expect from Cooper now that they'd made love. Men were odd creatures, she decided, and extremely territorial when they thought someone was sniffing around their turf. Considering his penchant for the caveman routine, anything was possible.

The chuckle that rumbled up from his chest when he shifted on the desk to look down at her was the last reaction she expected.

"You can't do this, Carly. I can't afford for you to do this. Besides, it's too little too late. I've decided to close the bar."

Well, this is certainly news, she thought, and frowned. He'd put his own money into the bar to keep it open because, as he'd claimed, The Wilde Side was all his uncle had and Hayden knew nothing else. She'd understood his reasons stemmed from the loyalty he felt for the man who'd raised him after his mother passed away, but what she couldn't fathom was his unexpected announcement to close The Wilde Side for good before seeing for himself that her plan had the potential for success.

"You can't do that," she said suddenly, wondering if his about-face stemmed from his inability to survive financially, or a loss of hope. "I've already hired the dancers, and we put those flyers up all over town. I even decided to take an ad out in the *Sun Times* this morning. It'll run on Wednesday, and in six days from today, The Wilde Side is going wild. You can't close the bar now."

"You said yesterday an ad was too expensive. And I sure didn't authorize an expenditure like that," he said, his voice rising again.

"Don't worry," she said in a placating tone. She stood and circled the desk. "I put it on my credit card, and you can pay me back after Thursday night. I have it all figured out."

"I'll just bet you do," he grumbled.

She chose to ignore that comment. "This is going to be a success, Cooper. You'll see."

He gave her a level stare. "And if it's not? Then what?"

"If not," she said with a shrug, as if spending over a thousand bucks for a group of male dancers was something she did all the time, "then I'll pay the guys for their time."

"Mind if I ask how much you agreed to pay them? The last time I checked, the bar was still my responsibility."

"One-fifty."

Cooper wasn't sure he heard her right. "Each?" he asked carefully. "A hundred and fifty dollars each?"

Her slow nod was all the confirmation he needed.

He took in a deep, long-suffering breath and invoked the gods for patience. She wasn't trying to help him make money; she was going to send him right into bankruptcy.

"Carly," he began, struggling to keep his voice calm. If he'd learned anything about Carly, it was that if he blustered, she'd simply jut her chin out at a stubborn angle and refuse to listen to reason. "In the past two years the bar has been lucky to clear more than three hundred bucks in a night. What makes you think it'll bring in enough to pay these guys just because of a little advertising?"

"This," she said, and reached across the desk for a yellow tablet filled with names. He took it from her and stared in surprise at the long list with numbers ranging from three to eight next to each of the names.

"These are reservations for Thursday," she explained. "Karen took most of these last night. This morning I even added three more parties to the list. We'll make money."

He continued to stare at the list in amazement. Even if Carly's plan worked, it didn't change the fact he still planned to close the bar. He really didn't want to continue living in an apartment close to fifty years old above an equally ancient bar that never saw a profit these days. Last night, he'd made a drastic mistake, one that could change his life in more ways than he'd anticipated.

The Wilde Side was the last place he wanted to raise children. Whether he and Carly had created a child last night remained to be seen, but he wanted better for any kid of his. The type of work he was trained for hardly qualified as nine to five, but at least it was more stable and a hell of a lot more wholesome than what he'd been raised around. A lot of his memories were happy ones, but he had enough bad ones to know he wanted better for his kid.

He should tell her about his plans, which were much more respectable than her crazy idea. He looked up from the list. The excitement and pleasure in her adorable eyes stopped him cold. She'd gone to great lengths in her struggle for independence, and he suspected her unorthodox plan was just one more step on her road to proving that she had what it took to be self-sufficient. No matter how spunky and fiery, there was insecurity behind the sass, and that made it tough for him to put a damper on her excitement or remind her she did have a safety net beneath her, whether or not she realized he was there to catch her should she fall.

She narrowed the space between them. Her hand landed on his knee and she stepped between his legs. "I'll make you a deal," she said, a sassy twinkle in her eyes as she looped her arms around his neck and wiggled closer.

"I've had about enough of your deals," he answered, settling his hands on the curve of her waist.

"If on Thursday night we don't make enough to pay the dancers *and* clear at least the same amount, I'll pay them myself and cover the cost of the ad."

He tried not to focus on the "we" in her offer, but he sure liked the sound of it coming from her. "That's a pretty big gamble you're willing to take," he said, wondering if he even possessed one iota of her strength and determination.

"It's like betting on a sure thing."

"There's no such thing as a sure thing. And have you forgotten that you can't afford it?"

She blew out a stream of breath that ruffled her feathery platinum bangs. "You have absolutely nothing to lose here, Cooper. Either way, you come out ahead. And if we do make money, which I'm positive we will, then you won't have to close down the bar."

"I don't like it," he said, keeping the fact that he'd already made up his mind to himself for just a while longer. She'd obviously put a lot of thought into this idea of hers, and he just didn't have the heart to disappoint her. *Has to be the defective gene at work,* he thought, and frowned.

"It's not costing you a dime. What's not to like?"

He eased his hands from her waist to cup her curvy bottom and pull her tighter against him. "When I came downstairs to help you paint, which is what I thought you were doing," he chastised her, "I found you with your hands all over some guy."

She had the audacity to toss her head back and laugh.

"I don't think it's so funny," he complained.

Her laughter stilled and she brushed her lips over his in a whisper of a kiss. "Those guys are harmless," she said, her eyes filled with a tenderness that made him nervous. "They're just a bunch of guys looking to make a little extra money. Most of them are in grad school and can use the bucks."

"I still don't have to like it."

A sassy grin curved her sweet mouth. "Does that mean you agree?"

Since she'd appeared out of nowhere a week ago dressed in a wedding gown, he'd made one bad choice after another, which had led him down a path he'd had no intention of taking. He didn't think agreeing to her new deal was going to be an improvement.

"Fine," he reluctantly agreed.

She pressed her body against his, making him give serious consideration to ignoring his responsibilities and carrying her upstairs to embark upon an exploration of her lush curves, instead. As much as he wanted to do nothing more, he refused to give in to the weakness shifting through him. He gently eased her away from him and stood, putting some much-needed distance between them.

He opened the door and held it for her. "Just don't think for a minute I'm leaving you alone with those young pups," he complained as she passed in front of him. If she was determined to teach a group of testosterone-filled grad students how to wiggle and shake, then she could damn well do it with him in the same room.

She looked over her shoulder at him as she sauntered down the corridor toward the main area of the bar and cast him one of those smiles filled with feminine satisfaction. "Don't tell me you're jealous?"

Unable to resist the urge to touch her one last time, he snagged her around the waist and pulled back her against him. He dipped his head to nuzzle the side of her neck. "You're damned right I am," he growled against her ear, feeling his own surge of male satisfaction when a delicate shiver passed through her.

"You have no reason to be jealous," she whispered, turning in his arms.

He rested his forehead against hers. "Oh yeah?"

"Yeah," she said, the teasing grin fading from her lips. "They're nice but..."

"But what?"

"But I'm not in love with them."

14

Rule 14: A lady must never allow her emotions to show.

CARLY COULDN'T really say what she had expected, but it certainly hadn't been the stark fear that had replaced the teasing light in Cooper's dark eyes when she'd so foolishly blurted out her feelings for him. Just because they'd made love didn't mean they were destined for happily ever after. And it certainly didn't mean she should have let Cooper in on her secret, either.

The bar was busy, busier than she'd hoped, but not enough that she didn't have time to dwell on the growing distance between them and how he'd done a bang-up job of avoiding anything remotely resembling intimacy for the past five days. He'd been so intent on avoiding her, he'd even left her to handle the bar during the day while he disappeared for hours, not returning until early evening, and without so much as a hint to his whereabouts.

She had taken advantage of the time alone, however. Her first order of business had been to update the jukebox with music from the current century. If she'd believed for a second he'd berate her for eliminating half the dinosaur rock selections, she couldn't have been more wrong. He hadn't even noticed.

Maybe that's what bothered her, she thought, propping her aching foot against the brass rung while she waited for him to finish filling a drink order. He hadn't noticed much of anything the past couple of days. At least nothing to do with her, and after the night they'd spent making love, her pride smarted something horrible.

He set the drinks on the circular tray and slid it toward her without comment. Their gazes connected for a split second, but he turned away, not even giving her the time to thank him for filling her order, since he'd moved on to the next one.

She lifted her chin as if Cooper and his sudden noninterest didn't matter and made her way through the crowded bar to deliver the drinks to a group of laughing women who appeared to be in their early fifties. Another twenty minutes and she'd have to leave Karen alone to handle the ever-increasing crowd of women while she organized her dancers for their second, and last, set of the night. She'd managed to coerce Benny and Joe into helping out with crowd management, and they'd taken their new roles as bouncers to heart, standing as still as palace guards in front of the section she'd roped off as a makeshift stage. No one dared get a little too friendly with any of her boys with a couple of scary-looking characters like Benny West and Joe Lanford standing guard.

"Excuse me, waitress?"

"Be right there," she called to the table behind her, while she finished taking a new order for fresh drinks. She promised the table of secretaries she'd have their drinks to them in a few minutes and turned around to take the next order.

"What'll it be, ladies?" she said, her pencil poised over the white scratch pad Karen suggested they use to keep track of orders. They'd expected a crowd thanks to the advance warning from the reservation list she and Karen had kept, but nothing could have prepared them for the standing-room-only crowd that had filled the room to near bursting. Her plan was a huge success. Too bad the victory felt so hollow.

When she received no response from the table, she looked up from her order pad and her heart sank clear to her toes. Smiling up at her were three pair of eyes in varying shades of blue. Well, Brenda and Chickie were smiling. Ali was doing her usual suspicion routine.

"What are you guys doing here?" she asked once she recovered from the initial shock of finding three of her six older sisters seated at the table. "And how did you find me?"

"Isn't that just like her?" Chickie said to Brenda. "Not so much as a 'How are you?' or 'Gee, it's good to see you.' You were raised better than that, Carly. What's happened to your manners?"

"I left them in Homer," Carly said, tucking the tray under her arm. "Seriously, what are you doing here?"

"Actually, we came here to ask you the same thing," Brenda said in that chastising tone she'd perfected over the years. As the oldest, she'd had plenty of practice.

Carly glanced over her shoulder toward Cooper, even if he was too busy mixing drinks to notice anything was wrong. "I don't have time right now," she said, deftly avoiding the subject for the time being. "Do you want something to drink?"

"We need to talk, Carly," Ali, the youngest of the three, said. She slid a lock of chin length honey-blond hair behind her ear. "We've all been worried about you."

"I know," Carly said around the huge, unexpected lump in her throat. "I'm sorry, but I really can't talk right now." She glanced around the room to make her point. "We're really busy."

Chickie drummed her fingers on the black lacquer table. "So we noticed."

"Do you guys want a drink or not?" Carly asked again. Despite the dread she felt knowing that her sisters had found her, her curiosity was running high, except she didn't have time to ask the multitude of questions flitting through her mind. Such as, how did they find her, and were they merely curious and concerned or had they come for some other reason—like convincing her to come home? "I have customers waiting."

The look the trio gave her spoke loud and clear. The reprieve granted would be a brief one, the interrogation definitely tabled until later. Chickie ordered mai tais for her and Brenda and clear soda for Ali. Carly promised to return soon with their order and escaped toward the bar, stopping to take two more orders along the way.

"What's wrong?" Karen asked, coming up to the bar with her own orders waiting to be filled. "You look like you've seen a ghost."

"Three of them," Carly murmured. At Karen's questioning look, she said, "My sisters are here."

"Really?" Karen craned her neck to scan the crowd. "Where?"

Carly pointed to the table in the far corner near the stage. "Over there. And I need you to do me a favor. Will you take this order to them when it's ready? Anything they want tonight is on me."

"Feeling guilty, eh?" Karen laughed.

Carly nodded truthfully, then disappeared into the storeroom she'd commandeered as a temporary backstage area for the guys. Other than Cooper's withdrawal, the night had been going so well, until now. Disaster loomed and she knew clear to her soul if her sisters had arrived with the intent of taking her home, Cooper wouldn't stand in her way.

And that hurt most of all.

The next three hours passed in a blur as Carly waited tables amid a crowd of women screaming encouragement to the dancers. At ten, the doors had opened to allow men into The Wilde Side. She'd been surprised at how many men had come, but realized Karen had been absolutely right in her prediction, even if she didn't quite agree with her philosophy. Bring in the women and the men were sure to follow, certain the women were ripe for the picking after being primed by ten good-looking, dancing bachelors.

She had managed a few snippets of conversation with her sisters throughout the night, but nothing that gleaned any solid information regarding their intent on coming to the city. Were they here merely to check up on her and assure themselves and report back that she was okay? Or did they have something more influential in mind, like taking her back to Homer? She had learned they'd located her general vicinity from the postmark on the postcard she'd mailed her parents, something she hadn't even thought of when she'd sent it. Once they knew which area to look in, considering all the flyers posted around the neighborhood with her name on them in conjunction with The Wilde Side, the rest was easy.

A little before 1:00 a.m., the crowd thinned substantially and business finally slowed, giving her more than a few minutes at a time to sit and talk with her sisters. After the initial shock of seeing them in a place like The Wilde Side passed, she acknowledged the fact that she'd actually missed them, even though she'd only been gone a couple of days shy of two weeks. She had spent her entire life with these women. Until she'd taken off, they'd always been there for her. That they were here now spoke volumes to Carly, and as much as she didn't want their interference in her decisions, she loved them for caring so much about her.

She carried a glass of cola to the table and sat beside Chickie. "It feels good to sit down," she admitted with a tired smile, dragging over a vacant chair from a nearby table to use as a footrest. Her feet ached, but the pain was well worth it, since the night had been such a huge success. According to Karen—Cooper couldn't be bothered to tell her himself—they pulled in more than enough money to pay the dancers and see a hefty profit. Cooper had kept the prices reasonable for mixed and blended drinks, and the women had kept ordering as Carly had predicted. A few more nights like this, and she suspected Cooper might actually reconsider his decision to close the bar for good.

Chickie slung her arm over her shoulders and gave her a gentle, comforting squeeze. "You look tired, kiddo."

Carly sighed and dropped her head against her sister's shoulder. "I am. But it feels good."

Brenda leveled her stark blue eyes on her. "So you gonna tell us what you're doing here?"

Carly considered Brenda's question for a moment before answering. She'd set out on a path of escape that had turned into one of self-discovery. She'd learned she could survive on her own, using her own wits and knowing there wasn't anyone to catch her and help set her back on the right path again should she fall. Making her own decisions and doing things her way was extremely liberating, but what had it gotten her? Nothing much besides a busted heart and a wounded ego. She couldn't even find a job that didn't include bartering for her room and board. In a city like Chicago, those skills, while helpful, wouldn't get her very far.

Her gaze slid to Cooper, busy, as he'd been all night, behind the bar. He, too, looked tired as he washed glasses in the large soapy tubs. Lines of fatigue bracketed his eyes and a weariness surrounded his mouth, which had been pretty much drawn and tight all evening long. Something was on his mind. Exactly what that something was, she didn't have a clue since he'd hardly spoken to her all week.

She turned her attention back to Brenda and straightened. "Finding myself?" she answered with a hesitant shrug.

Ali rolled her eyes in exasperation. "That is so self-indulgent, Carly."

"Not to mention very eighties," Chickie added in good humor, folding her hands on the tabletop.

"Why'd you run away like that?" Ali asked, leaning forward. "We've all been so worried about you."

"I'm sorry," Carly said, shifting her gaze from Brenda to Ali. "I couldn't go through with the wedding."

"Obviously," Brenda said dryly. "But running away was a bit extreme."

Carly set her soda on the table with a snap. "I tried to tell Dean," she argued. "He wouldn't listen. He—"

"We know," Chickie interrupted, settling her hands over Carly's. "Jilly told us."

"How did Dean take it?" Carly asked. She dreaded the answer, but needed to know he was all right. She truly cared about him, and hurting him was never her intention. But caring about someone and being in love with him enough to spend the rest of her life with him were two different issues, in her opinion.

The other three Cassidy women looked at each other, then back at Carly. "What?" Carly asked when they wouldn't answer. "He's okay, isn't he?"

Brenda let out a long breath. "Yes, Carly. He's fine."

"His pride was a bit wounded, but I think it's been salvaged," Chickie chimed in with a chuckle.

Carly frowned. "Salvaged? What do you mean salvaged?"

A grin tipped Ali's mouth. "Maybe soothed is a better word."

"Well," Chickie said, "the honeymoon trip was paid in full. I guess it really did seem a shame to let a ten-day vacation go to waste."

"It wasn't like you expected a refund, right?" Brenda asked her.

Carly leaned back and crossed her arms, looking at each of her sisters. "What exactly are you trying to say?"

"Dean went to the Keys," Ali said, and looked away.

"And?" Carly prompted, certain there was more to this than Dean being smart enough to make use of the honeymoon trip they'd planned.

"And," Brenda said, "he took Abigail Copely with him."

Carly stared at her sister. "The dog catcher?"

Brenda nodded briskly, a silky lock of golden-blond hair falling across her forehead. "She'd be the one."

Dean and Abigail Copely? She knew Abigail casually, someone to say hello to if they passed on the street. The dog catcher had only recently moved to Homer and was a member of her father's congregation.

She never suspected Abigail had a thing for *her* fiancé. Her former fiancé, she amended. "But I didn't... They weren't...were they?"

"No!" Chickie offered quickly, sensing where Carly was going with her unasked question. "From the rumors we heard, Abigail was in the park trying to catch Mrs. Green's Yorkshire terrier again when she ran into Dean, who'd gone for a walk after he...well, after you, uh...left. The next thing we heard, she went with him to the Keys."

So much for her groom being heartbroken over her abrupt departure. The momentary stab to her pride faded quickly. Dean was a good man and deserved happiness with the right woman, one who'd love him as he deserved to be loved. If Abigail Copely was that woman, then Carly was happy for them both.

Too bad her own happiness was so short-lived.

"I'm sorry that I put everyone though so much trouble," she said. "Were Mom and Dad upset about the wedding? It was my fault everything was ruined, so I plan to pay them back."

Ali sipped her soda and actually grinned. Again. "That was taken care of, too."

Carly's eyes rounded in surprise. "Dean married the dog catcher?"

"No," Brenda said with a laugh. "Jilly and Morgan took your place."

"Serious?" After the horrendous engagement to Owen Kramer, Carly had been surprised to learn that Jill was even contemplating marriage again. Of course, Morgan was adorable and sweet and obviously head over heels in love with her sister.

"Oh yeah," Chickie supplied. "It wasn't legal until Monday after the church ceremony because they had to get a marriage license and have it officiated by a justice of the peace, but they did have a wedding, and a reception."

Ali gave her a narrowed look. "You should have been there, Carly. We actually had a good time."

Carly shot a tolerant glance at her sister, a skill she'd obviously adopted from Cooper, before asking, "Did they go back to California?"

"They'll be home for the family reunion picnic," Chickie answered, then gave her a look filled with a wealth of meaning. "We're hoping the *entire* family will be home for that."

Carly sighed. Yes, she was certain the family did expect her to be home soon. Whether or not she stayed in Chicago depended on Cooper, and if the past few days were any indication, she had a feeling she'd be packing her meager belongings in the morning and driving back to her hometown.

Her gaze slid to Cooper again. He stood behind the bar talking to Karen and Vinny, the med student and now part-time dancer at The Wilde Side, who'd been flirting and laughing with Karen most of the night. Cooper must have felt her gaze on him, because he focused those intense eyes on her.

Her heart stuttered, and her pulse rate picked up speed, all from a look. She had it bad. Real bad. But what good was bad if Cooper didn't return her feelings? He'd made that patently clear with his stellar avoidance tactics.

"Carly?" Ali prodded when Carly continued to look in Cooper's direction. "Who is he?"

"What I want to know is, who is he to you?" Brenda asked quietly.

Could she keep no secrets from her sisters? Reluctantly, she waved him over, and he signaled he'd be there in a minute. The least she could do was introduce them to the man who'd managed to shatter her heart in a matter of days.

"Well?" Chickie prodded. "I've seen that look before, Carly. We've all had it."

"He's just..." Just what? A friend? A lover? How could she tell her sisters he was the man who could look clear down to her soul and knew instinctively just how to touch her emotionally? He was the one who'd stolen her heart. The one who'd so carelessly tossed her love aside and refused to even acknowledge his own feelings for her.

She knew he cared for her. He hadn't said the words, but she knew, just as she knew he feared following in the footsteps of his uncle and mother. Regardless of what she'd told him the night they'd made love, he couldn't or wouldn't forget his past.

Brenda reached across the table and squeezed her hand. "Just what, Carly?"

"Just a guy," she managed, blinking back the sudden moisture accumulating in her gaze. Unable or unwilling to share that part of her life with her sisters, she wasn't sure, but her time with Cooper was special. Special, and a little too hurtful for her to talk about with them. Keeping secrets in a house full of women was unheard of, but just this once, she wanted to hold her memories close to her heart. At least for a while.

He stepped from behind the bar and sauntered over to the table. A smile she hadn't seen in days tipped his mouth. Faded denim hugged his lean hips and long, muscular legs, and he wore a deep brown polo shirt that matched the color of his eyes and emphasized his finely honed body to perfection.

Chickie let out a soft whistle of approval.

Carly elbowed her sister.

"Cooper, I'd like you to meet my sisters," she said, and introduced him to each of them. The congenial smile canting his oh-so-sexy mouth didn't waver when he shook their hands and managed a little idle chitchat before politely excusing himself. Unfortunately, she knew him well enough to recognize the expression banked in his eyes as resignation.

The man gave off more mixed signals than a faulty radio transmitter. He'd barely acknowledged her presence for days, and now he had the nerve to give her an "I told you so" look. Just because her family had arrived, didn't mean she was returning to Homer. She could stay in Chicago. If she had a reason to stay.

If *Cooper* gave her a reason to stay.

"It's time for last call," she said, and swung her feet to the floor.

Chickie put her hand on Carly's shoulder before she could escape. "Come back to Homer with us, Carly."

Carly let out a long breath. She'd known they'd come to convince her to return home. What had she accomplished in the past two weeks? She still had no job, no apartment and—she glanced in Cooper's direction—no relationship. Not that she'd exactly planned on the latter, but the truth remained that she'd fallen hard for him. She couldn't make sense out of her feelings for Cooper any more than she could understand the intricate theory of relativity. Still, if he gave her one inkling of hope, she'd gladly tell her sisters she'd be home for a visit over the holidays because she belonged in Chicago with the man she loved.

She looked at them. "Are you staying in the city tonight?"

Brenda nodded. "We'll be at the Marriott."

Carly bit her lower lip and glanced in Cooper's direction one last time before turning back to face her sisters. "If I'm not there by noon," she said, hoping she was making the right choice, "then I won't be coming."

Worry filled Ali's pale blue eyes. "Carly, are you sure? Is this really what you want?"

Carly blinked back the moisture clouding her gaze and shrugged. "I think so."

"Is *he* who you want?" Chickie slipped a wayward curl from Carly's face and tucked it behind her ear. Leave it to Chickie, the most romantic of the Cassidy girls, to get to the heart of the matter.

Carly gave Chickie a wavering grin. "I know he is," she said. Now all she had to do was convince Cooper.

15

Rule 15: When a gentleman makes his honorable intentions clear, it is no longer necessary for a lady to play hard to get.

COOPER SLIPPED the last of the cash into the cloth bag and tucked it inside the safe. He spun the lock, unable to comprehend how in one night the bar had made more money than it had in the six months since he'd been running the place. According to the ledgers and bank statements, for nearly two years the bar had been operating in the red, and one night would bring it close to the black once again.

He knew the answer. It was simple, he thought, closing and locking the door to the office. Carly. Her methods might have been off the wall, but he couldn't remember the last time a standing-room-only crowd had filled The Wilde Side, if ever. Too bad he'd decided to close the bar, because she'd definitely found a fool-proof plan to keep it up and running with her idea for a weekly ladies' night.

He walked into the open area of the bar, lit only by the neon signs hung along the newly painted walls. He sensed her presence, his radar tracking her down with little effort as he peered into the semidarkness and found her standing near the jukebox.

Her hands were braced on the glass as she kept her head bent examining the selections, her delicate features illuminated by the soft blue Coors Light beer sign above her. He quietly moved to one of the bar stools and sat, just watching her. Letting her go was going to be one of the toughest things he'd ever done, but he had no other choice unless he was willing to relinquish himself to her completely.

Carly would accept no less than all of him.

All was more than he had to give.

As much as he'd thought about their situation the past few days, he'd come to the conclusion saying goodbye to her was inevitable, and the best thing for both of them. She had a family who loved her and he had virtually nothing to offer her. Maybe in another time or another place, something more could have emerged. Despite the unexplainable connection he felt with her, now that her family had found her, the inevitable would come a lot sooner than he'd anticipated.

She made a selection and the jukebox whirred to life, the speakers placed strategically throughout the bar filling with the soft, romantic melody of a country music ballad. She turned, her expressive turquoise eyes widening in surprise. "I didn't hear you come in," she said, slowly walking toward him.

"Thank you, Carly."

She stopped a few feet away, propping her backside against the pool table. "What are you thanking me for?"

"Tonight. You were right. We made a killing," he said with a smile he was far from feeling.

She returned his grin with one of her own that failed to light up her eyes the way he liked. "I could say I told you so," she teased, even if her voice lacked its usual lighthearted quality.

She glanced away. When she turned her gaze back to

his, he saw pain and confusion, and blamed himself for putting those emotions there. "Will you continue with ladies' night?"

After I'm gone.

She didn't say the words, but Cooper felt them hanging between them just the same. "I'm still closing the bar soon."

"Oh." She pushed herself up onto the ledge of the pool table and crossed her legs. "What about your uncle?"

He zeroed in on the bare flesh, itching to touch her, to skim his hands up her legs and beneath the hem of her tan shorts, to make her his one last time. Making love to her now wouldn't change anything. He still had responsibilities and couldn't afford her special brand of distraction. And she still had family waiting for her.

He shrugged, then stuffed his fingers in the front pockets of jeans. "If he shows up before then, it'll be his decision. As long as I'm in charge, the decision and responsibility are mine, and I'm closing it down."

"Even after the success we...you had tonight? It seems silly when—"

"It's not what I want, Carly," he said abruptly. He couldn't help noticing *we* wasn't a part of her vocabulary any longer. "It never has been."

She laid her arms over her crossed legs and looked up at him. "What *do* you want, Cooper?" she asked.

The wariness in her voice made him feel like a first-class jerk. Caution was a foreign concept to Carly, and he hated that he was the one to add hesitancy to her repertoire. The part of him guaranteed to head straight into heartache and disaster longed to tell her he wanted her the way he'd never wanted another woman, and probably never would again. If he'd gotten anything out of the past two weeks with Carly, it was solid proof he was no better than the rest of the Wildes. The fact that he'd lost such complete control the night they'd made love was enough of a reminder. He'd taken risks neither one of them could afford, something he never would have done if he'd been in control. Carly demanded he give up that control and he had, leaving him no choice but to say goodbye to her now to save his own hide later.

Or his heart?

He didn't like the answer.

"Are your sisters waiting for you?" he asked, avoiding her question.

She sighed and straightened, her expression evidence enough that she wasn't fooled in the least by his abrupt change of subject. "They're staying in the city tonight. I told them if I didn't meet them by noon at their hotel, to go on without me."

She slid off the pool table and slowly walked toward him, determination apparent in every step.

"I see," he said.

"I don't have to go with them, Cooper." She took the last step separating them and looked into his eyes, clear down to his lying soul.

He gently smoothed his thumb down her satiny cheek. "Yes, Princess. You do."

Carly briefly closed her eyes against the pain, willing the tears not to fall in front of Cooper. Her plea was useless, and she attempted to blink back the moisture blurring her vision.

"Can you at least tell me why?" she asked around the solid lump in her throat. "I thought we had...I dunno...something special, I guess. Was I wrong?"

He let out a breath and lowered his hand. He looked

away, and she couldn't help hoping that he couldn't bear to look at her and see the pain he caused her. Pain she couldn't claim as his sole responsibility.

He lifted his gaze to hers, a hardness in the dark depths she suspected was feigned to protect himself. "I already told you I have nothing to offer you."

She shook her head. "You're talking material—"

"No," he cut her off and stood. "*I* have nothing to offer you."

He wasn't referring to material possessions. This wasn't about a job or a place to live, but something much more important. Because of who she was, he was referring to something any relationship between them would never survive without, and something he wasn't willing to give. Himself.

She pulled in a shaky breath. "So I guess this is it, then. I'm going back to Homer to teach music and you're..." She laughed, the sound bitter and caustic even to her. She turned away and headed toward the back stairs that would lead her to his apartment. "God only knows what you'll be doing," she muttered to herself. "Probably breaking some poor girl's heart."

His hand clamped on her arm and he gently spun her around to face him. "Carly, look—"

She tugged her arm free. "No, Cooper. Don't." She couldn't take anymore. A sob shook her and she cursed herself for crying in front of him.

She'd come to Chicago looking for something, and what she'd found was so much more than she'd ever anticipated. She'd found the very reason she'd run off in the first place. She'd finally found love, the real kind that lasted. The kind of love her parents had even after forty years of marriage.

What good had her grand discovery done her? She'd

found it, and now it was being withheld from her before she had a chance to experience the full emotional impact of true love.

"Don't try to make it all better," she told him. "It's too little, too late."

"I never wanted to hurt you," he said, a trace of pain in his voice.

She received no satisfaction from the fact he was hurting, as well. The emotion lacing his smooth, velvet voice only sent the truth home: unless Cooper could overcome the demons of his past and realize he was nothing like his mother or uncle, they would have no future.

She reached for the door and stopped. "I never wanted to get hurt, either, Cooper. But I did."

With one last look into those gorgeous eyes, she walked away, leaving her heart and her hopes for the future behind.

COOPER LOOKED around the empty apartment and never felt more alone. For the past three weeks there'd been no sneakers left in the living room for him to trip over. No newspapers spread over the sofa or coffee rings on the table. The cap was always on the toothpaste right where he'd left it, and he hadn't had to navigate his way through a dangling sea of satin and lace to get to the shower every morning.

Worse, there was no sassy woman around to disrupt his orderly life or distract him from his responsibilities.

He didn't bother to fold the Sunday paper, but tossed it carelessly in the recycle bin. Instead of carrying his coffee mug into the kitchen to rinse and set in the dishwasher, he left it on the dining table. Neither act of rebellion helped fill the void nor worked to ease the pain that had settled in his chest.

Who was he kidding? The pain had settled over his heart, and as far as he was concerned, only one cure existed.

Hayden still hadn't returned, but he'd finally decided to get in touch with Cooper. Without so much as an apology for taking off again, he'd informed his nephew he'd taken the plunge and was enjoying the benefits of wedded bliss. With Hayden's blessing now that the elder Wilde had decided to retire to Florida with his bride, three days ago Cooper had closed the doors to The Wilde Side for good.

Thanks to Carly's ingenuity, he'd continued with ladies' night for two more weeks and had garnered enough cash to cover the outstanding invoices, pay Karen a hefty two-month severance package and recoup some of his own money he'd put into the bar. A week ago Karen had informed him she'd accepted a job at Cook County General in the emergency department while she went back to school to finish up her nursing degree.

This morning the real estate agent had placed a For Sale sign on the old brownstone. He'd recently accepted a new position as a security systems analyst, a job that would take him all over the country for days at a time. He could live just about anywhere he wanted. *Anywhere* wasn't near Carly.

He hadn't heard from her, which left him operating under the assumption a pregnancy hadn't resulted from the night they'd spent together. He hadn't expected disappointment would be the perfect accompaniment to the pain and loneliness he'd been carrying around as his constant companions since Carly walked out on him.

"No less than you deserved," he muttered to himself as he stalked into the bedroom. He pulled a duffel bag from the closet and tossed in a few clothes. He'd been too blind and stubborn to give her a reason to stay. Carly was chaotic and unique, and he'd foolishly expected her to fit into a neat, orderly compartment in his life. Only she didn't, and probably never would. Instead, she came crashing through on an emotional roller coaster and expected him to hang on and take the wild ride with her.

And he'd been too afraid to enjoy the ride.

With the clarity of hindsight heightened by too many sleepless nights since he'd let her walk out of his life without a fight, he understood it wasn't her he feared, but how she refused to accept nothing less than everything he had to give. He believed if he gave, he'd lose himself, and that's where he'd made his error in judgment. By giving, he had everything to gain; Carly's love and every blissful moment he could capture with a woman who grabbed every moment with both hands and embraced the clutter, and reveled in the mystery and chaos.

After making certain Hercules had enough food and water for the night, he left the apartment and headed toward the small town of Homer. Whether or not Carly would even speak to him when he arrived was a gamble, but he refused to give up this time.

This time he really did have too much to lose; the woman who'd demanded his soul and hadn't bothered to give it back when she'd left.

CARLY USUALLY enjoyed the family reunion picnic, but this one was different. This year her heart just wasn't in the festivities. Probably because she'd left it back in Chicago with a man too stupid to see what was right in front of him.

She let out a frustrated breath as she did every time she thought about Cooper, then shifted on the plaid blanket spread beneath the shade of an ancient oak. A book she pretended to read but couldn't concentrate on if her life depended on it lay open on her lap.

"Sweetheart, aren't you going to eat something?"

Carly looked up and smiled at her father. "Maybe later."

Reverend Richard Cassidy moved aside a plastic bucket and shovel and sat next to Carly on the blanket. "Nice day for the picnic," he said, shielding his eyes from the sun as he searched the immediate area.

"Hmm," Carly murmured, attempting to focus on the unread pages.

He waved to his grandchildren playing on the swing set. "Jill and Morgan called last night. Your sister is trying a high profile criminal case on her own next month."

Carly snapped the book closed and looked over at her father. The man was up to something. In his own unique way and in his own good time, Richard Cassidy was about to impart advice in a way his daughters had come to expect. He didn't pry, he didn't make demands on his daughters, but he had a way of letting them know when something wasn't quite the way it should be.

"What's your point, Dad?"

"Oh, no point," her father said in that sly way of his. "I was merely commenting on Jilly's latest career achievement. She's very happy, you know."

Carly tossed the book aside. "She should be. Morgan's one of the good guys." She still believed Cooper was, too. Sweet Mary, she missed him. She'd give just about anything to see him one more time. To look into those intense eyes, to feel his arms around her, to taste his lips, to feel his hands as they...

"Just so he makes Jill happy," her father said, intruding on Carly's thoughts. "I'm proud of Jill. She wanted something and she went for it."

Carly crossed her legs. "Dad, you have a point. Would get to it please?"

The reverend smiled and smoothed his hand over Carly's curls. "What do you want?"

Carly shook her head. "Ah, now we get to the heart of the matter." She shrugged. "To be happy, I guess."

Concern filled her father's eyes. "But you're not, are you, sweetheart?"

Carly looked away. No, she wasn't happy. It'd be a long time before she enjoyed that elusive emotion. "No," she admitted. She'd told her parents almost everything about Cooper, and they'd offered her comfort and understanding instead of the chastisement she'd expected. For that, she loved them. The last thing she'd wanted to hear was how foolish she'd been when her heart still ached from his final rejection.

Her father took her hand and momentarily held it between his own. "Your sisters never let anyone prevent them from living their lives the way they wanted. What makes you think you're so different?"

Her father's intuition always amazed her and was no doubt the reason his congregation adored him. As kids, they rarely got away with anything because somehow, someway, their father always knew when his daughters were in trouble.

"Everyone is always trying to tell me how to live my life, for one," she told him. "I shouldn't go here, or I should take this subject in school, or it'd be better if I accept this job and lived close to home. All I wanted to do was make my own decisions. My own choices."

"And when you did, the world didn't come to an end, either, did it?"

A rueful grin tugged Carly's lips. "My methods of execution leave a little to be desired."

Richard smiled lovingly at his daughter. "You have to do what's going to make you happy. No one can tell you what that is, Carly."

"I know." She leaned back on her hands and surveyed the picnic grounds. Dusk would be setting soon. Her nieces and nephews would need to be taken home shortly, to be bathed and put to bed.

"Do you?" he asked cryptically as he stood.

Carly watched as her father crossed the picnic area to the playground to watch his grandchildren play. Did she? Did she really know what would make her happy?

She looked around the area again and frowned when a black Ford, short-bed pickup pulled into the parking lot in the distance. She waited for the occupant to emerge, a slow smile spreading across her face when she caught sight of those wide shoulders and lean hips she'd never be able to forget.

Oh yes, she did know what would make her happy, and if his presence in Homer was any indication, he'd finally realized it for himself.

Every instinct inside her clamored for her to charge to her feet and run as fast she could into Cooper's arms. Instead, she decided to practice a little restraint for once in her life. She grabbed her book and quickly opened it again, biting her lower lip until a shadow fell across her.

She looked up into that handsome face, the same one that had been haunting her dreams for the past three weeks, making sleep darn near impossible. He looked haggard around the edges and tired, but she didn't take any comfort in the fact he'd been suffering, too. Neither one of them should have been suffering. They should have been enjoying each other.

"Hi," he said, his smooth voice music to her ears.

"You lost?" she asked, forcing her gaze back to the book in her lap.

He crouched beside her and she breathed in his scent. "Not anymore."

She squeezed her eyes shut and counted to five so she wouldn't cry. "Really?" she managed, surprised her voice wasn't trembling half as much as her insides were. "Found yourself a map, huh?"

He cleared his throat and reached for her book. "These are a little easier to read this way," he said, his voice infused with humor as he turned her book around right side up.

"So what are you doing here, Wilde? Surely you didn't drive all the way to Homer to show me how to read a book."

He pulled off his sunglasses and slipped them in the pocket of his white T-shirt. "I missed you."

Missing her was a start, but not what she wanted to hear. "I missed you, too. Now that we've established we've grown accustomed to each other, was there something in particular you wanted?"

"You're not going to make this easy, are you?"

She scrambled to her feet and shot what she hoped was a careless glance over her shoulder as she walked away. "What do you think?" she said, and headed to the picnic tables. Her appetite had returned with a vengeance.

He swore and hurried after her. Snagging her wrist, he pulled her around to face him. "I more than missed you," he admitted.

She tugged her hand from his grasp. "You're getting warmer."

He muttered something she didn't quite catch while shoving his hands through his short, sable hair.

She walked away again.

"Dammit, Carly," he shouted after her. "I love you. Now will you stand still?"

She stopped and turned back to face him. Her family had gathered not far behind her, but she didn't care. Cooper was all that mattered to her right now.

She crossed her arms and tilted her head slightly to the side as she looked him up and down. Sweet Mary, the man was gorgeous. And he loved her.

"It took you long enough to figure it out. I hope you're not always this slow-witted, Cooper. I'd like to think our children would be a little quicker on the uptake."

He planted his hands on his hips. "We'll never have any if you keep walking away all the time."

She ignored the snickers and giggles behind her and took a few steps closer to Cooper. "How many?"

Love softened his gaze and a sexy grin tipped his mouth. "However many you can handle, Princess."

"I like the sound of that," she murmured quietly, closing the distance between them and slipping into his arms.

He held her close, next to his heart, a place he'd kept

closed off from her. A place she planned to reside for the next sixty or so years.

"Silly man," she said, wreathing her arms around his neck. "Didn't you know you never stood a chance against a woman smart enough to establish her own laws?"

"What laws?" he asked, slipping his arms around her waist.

A contented little sigh escaped her. Cooper's arms wasn't a place she ever planned to tire of being. "Carly's Law," she told him. "Never settle for anything less than all of you."

He gently brushed his lips over hers in a kiss softer than a whisper. "You've got it. Heart, body and soul, Princess."

"I never doubted it for a minute," she said, lifting her face for one of those toe-curling kisses that would be hers for the rest of her life.

_____ Epilogue _____

Carly's Law: Happily ever after isn't just for fairy tales.

Sixteen Months Later...

"ARE YOU SURE he's coming, Carly?"

Carly pulled the apple crisp from the oven and set it on the counter to cool. "He'll be here," she told Ali, then checked the watermelon-shaped clock she'd given her mother for Christmas when she was ten. "He called this morning before he left Miami and should have arrived at O'Hare nearly an hour ago."

Chickie turned off the tap and set the last of the potatoes she'd been washing on the towel to dry. "Let's just hope he makes it before the storm hits," she said, picking up a potato peeler and handing it to Jill.

"It's after one already. It'd be a shame if he missed Thanksgiving dinner," Jill added from her place at the big kitchen table. She propped her feet up on another chair to keep them from swelling and took the peeler from Chickie.

Wendy handed Brenda the last of the large glass bowls in the cabinet and climbed down from the step stool. "I'm just glad you could make it," she said. "Since you and Cooper moved to New York, we never get to see you."

Carly rolled her eyes. Even moving to New York didn't stop her family from keeping tabs on her. She heard from at least one of her sisters on a weekly basis, and she called her parents every other weekend. As much as she'd craved her independence, she never imagined she'd suffer from homesickness, but after nine months in the city, she still had the occasional pang or two. Not that she'd tell them. The last thing her sisters needed was a reason to gloat or chime in with a series of I-told-you-so's.

"My new show is opening New Year's Day," she told them, "and I've been busy in meetings and rehearsals." Her job as an assistant choreographer for one of New York's top production companies kept her busy, which helped ease the loneliness on those days when Cooper had to leave town for any length of time.

Carly opened the cabinet for a mixing bowl and started adding the ingredients for the Waldorf salad that Lisa had been busy chopping. "Give Jill a hard time for a change," she told them. "She lives in California and doesn't come home all that often, either."

Jill plucked the potato peel from her rounded tummy and tossed it into the garbage can. "You're the baby, Carly. It's expected."

"She's right," Ali added, lifting her son from the high chair. "And Jill and Morgan have been home more than you lately, so I wouldn't push my luck if I were you, Baby Sister."

Carly blew out a stream of breath and dumped a box of raisins into the salad. Was it her fault she and Cooper were both busy with their jobs? She kept the question to herself knowing how they'd answer, with an extremely vocal *Yes!*

"And where is Morgan?" Carly asked Jill. "I haven't seen him since this morning."

"He, Brad and Ron are with Dad and Grandpa setting up the manger scene on the church lawn."

Carly laughed. "You mean the guys are setting it up while Dad and Grandpa argue over how it should be done."

"That about covers it," Chickie added as Jill set another peeled potato into the large pot of water.

"If they don't get back soon, *they'll* miss Thanksgiving dinner," Jill said. She stopped peeling and looked around the kitchen. "Hey, isn't someone going to help me with these? I've got at least ten pounds of potatoes here, and Junior and I can't do them all by ourselves."

"You've done nothing but give orders since you got here," Brenda teased.

"I'm pregnant. I can get away with it." To Carly, she asked, "How's Cooper's job going?"

Carly added dressing to the salad and tossed. "Better than we thought it would, actually. He still has to travel some, but moving to New York has helped keep him home more often since the main office is in Manhattan and that's where a lot of their clients are based."

Brenda snagged an extra peeler from the drawer and sat at the table with Jill. "I don't know why anyone would want to live in New York City."

"Don't knock it till you've tried it, Brenda," Carly said, adding a dash of salt to the Waldorf salad.

"You don't really plan to raise a family in that city, do you?" Jill asked her.

Coming from Jill, the question was odd considering she and Morgan lived in Los Angeles. "There's nothing wrong with 'that city,'" she told Jill. "We've already decided we'll move to the suburbs when the time comes."

That time was coming a lot sooner than either of them expected. She'd received the confirmation the day before she flew back home for Thanksgiving weekend that she was indeed pregnant. She was dying to tell Coop, but he'd been on a security job in Miami, which allowed him to spend a couple of days with his uncle before flying into Chicago to spend the long weekend with her family. Telling a man he was going to be a father wasn't something she wanted to do over the telephone.

The urge to share the happy news with her sisters was strong, but she forced herself into silence until she could tell Cooper. *If* he ever arrived.

Thirty minutes later, the unsuspecting father-to-be walked into the kitchen looking stunningly gorgeous in a charcoal suit and loosened paisley tie. They'd only been married a little under a year, and one sweep of those eyes still had the power to make her tingle all over.

"Something smells great," he said, setting his overnight bag and trench coat on one of the empty chairs.

Carly tossed the pot holders aside to cross the kitchen and slip into her husband's arms. "I hope that's my perfume you're referring to, Wilde," she said, looping her arms around his neck and planting a welcome-home kiss on his sexy mouth.

"No," he said and shook his head, a teasing light entering his warm gaze. "It's whatever's in the oven."

"I missed you," she whispered, then slipped her arms from around his neck to take hold of his hand. "Excuse us, ladies," she told her sisters, and pulled Cooper as far away from prying ears and ribald comments as she could get considering the house was overflowing with four generations of Cassidys.

"I didn't get to say hello to everyone," he complained, following behind her.

She stopped at the stairs. Children's laughter carried

from the upper level. Was there nowhere in this house for them to be alone? "You can be congenial later."

She spied the open door to her father's study down the hallway. "This way," she said, and tugged his hand again so he'd follow.

He laughed, the sound deep and rich. "Carly, what's going on?"

"Is it a crime to want to be alone with my husband after not seeing him for four whole days?"

"Four days," he said, closing the door to her father's study and pulling her into his arms at the same time. "Not four months."

"Well it's a good thing," she said, breathing in his intoxicating scent, "because four months from now you wouldn't recognize me."

She waited for her hint to register. When all he did was frown and give her a look filled with confusion, she rolled her eyes. "Cooper, in four months I'll be about six months along."

He shrugged, still not catching on. "Along with what?"

"God, help me," she muttered. "Pregnant, Cooper. We're going to have a baby."

"Oh. That." He dipped his head to nuzzle her neck. She angled her head to give him better access.

Oh that?

She pulled back and searched his face for any inkling of emotion. Finding none, she frowned. "'Oh, that' is all you have to say?"

His big, warm hands slid up her back and over her shoulders, stopping when he cupped her face in his palms. He held her still, his mouth far too many inches from hers. "Princess, do you really think I don't know every inch of your delicious body?"

She narrowed her eyes. "You didn't have a clue, Cooper. Admit it."

The smile that tipped his mouth was as breathtaking as his kisses. "I checked messages from the airport in Miami after I called you. The Women's Health Center called and wants you to schedule your first prenatal appointment next week."

"Are you happy about this?" she asked. "About starting our own family so soon? Our lives are going to change. A lot."

He'd come a long way from the man who'd nearly turned his back on her because he feared losing himself if he gave in to the love he felt. Cooper tended to resist change, and she couldn't help the tiny stab of concern that he might see a baby as another disruption to his life. A life he'd pretty much given up hope of keeping as neat and orderly as when she'd first met him.

She never doubted Cooper, or his love for her, but every once in a while she'd detect a hint of fear in his eyes, usually when they were surrounded by her loud, boisterous family, but it only lasted for a few seconds. Cooper had been an only child, and she had to give him credit. Regardless of how overwhelming the Cassidys could be, he'd adjusted quite well.

His mouth brushed hers in a featherlight kiss. "What's a little more chaos in my life so long as I have you to share it with?"

Pressing her body against his, she angled her head and kissed him. He deepened the kiss, and she felt all the love and emotion inside him.

She really had found more than she'd bargained for when she'd taken a walk on the wild side. She'd found Cooper. All of him.

Some secrets are better left buried...

Yesterday's Scandal by

WILKINS

A mysterious stranger has come to town...

Former cop Mac Cordero was going undercover one last time to
find and exact revenge on the man who fathered, then abandoned
him. All he knew was that the man's name was McBride—a name,
that is synonymous with scandal.

...and he wants her!

Responsible, reliable Sharon Henderson was drawn to the sexy-as-
sin stranger. She couldn't help falling for him hard and fast. Then
she discovered that their love was based on a lie....

YOU WON'T WANT TO MISS IT!

On sale September 2000 at your favorite retail outlet.

HARLEQUIN®
Makes any time special ™

If you enjoyed what you just read,
then we've got an offer you can't resist!

Take 2 bestselling love stories FREE!

Plus get a FREE surprise gift!

**Don't miss
an exciting opportunity
to save on the purchase of
Harlequin and Silhouette books!**

Buy any two Harlequin or
Silhouette books and save
$10.00 off future Harlequin
and Silhouette purchases

OR

buy any three
Harlequin or Silhouette books
and save **$20.00 off** future
Harlequin and Silhouette purchases.

*Watch for details
coming in October 2000!*

PHQ400

HARLEQUIN®
*M*akes any time special ™

Silhouette®
Where love comes alive™

HARLEQUIN
Duets™

Pick up a Harlequin Duets™ from August–October 2000 and receive $1.00 off the original cover price. *

Experience the "lighter side of love" in a Harlequin Duets™.
This unbeatable value just became irresistible with our special introductory price of $4.99 U.S./$5.99 CAN. for 2 Brand-New, Full-Length Romantic Comedies.

Offer available for a limited time only.
Offer applicable only to Harlequin Duets™.
*Original cover price is $5.99 U.S./$6.99 CAN.

Visit us at www.eHarlequin.com   HDMKD

HARLEQUIN®

makes any time special—online...

your romantic
life

➤ Talk to Dr. Romance, find a romantic recipe, or send a virtual hint to the love of your life. You'll find great articles and advice on romantic issues that are close to your heart.

your romantic
books

➤ Visit our *Author's Alcove* and try your hand in the Writing Round Robin—contribute a chapter to an online book in the making.

➤ Enter the *Reading Room* for an interactive novel—help determine the fate of a story being created now by one of your favorite authors.

➤ Drop into *Shop eHarlequin* to buy the latest releases— read an excerpt, find this month's Harlequin top sellers.

your romantic
escapes

➤ Escape into romantic movies at *Reel Love*, learn what the stars have in store for you with *Lovescopes*, treat yourself to our *Indulgences Guides* and get away to the latest romantic hot spots in *Romantic Travel*.

All this and more available at
www.eHarlequin.com
on Women.com Networks

HECHAN1R